FIRED UP
FOR BATTLE
2 GRAPHIC ADVENTURES

Adapted by
Simcha Whitehill

An Imprint of
Scholastic

ISBN 978-1-339-02806-4

10 9 8 7 6 5 4 3 2 1   24 25 26 27 28

Printed in China   62

First printing 2024

Designed by Cheung Tai

CONTENTS

A Legendary Trial

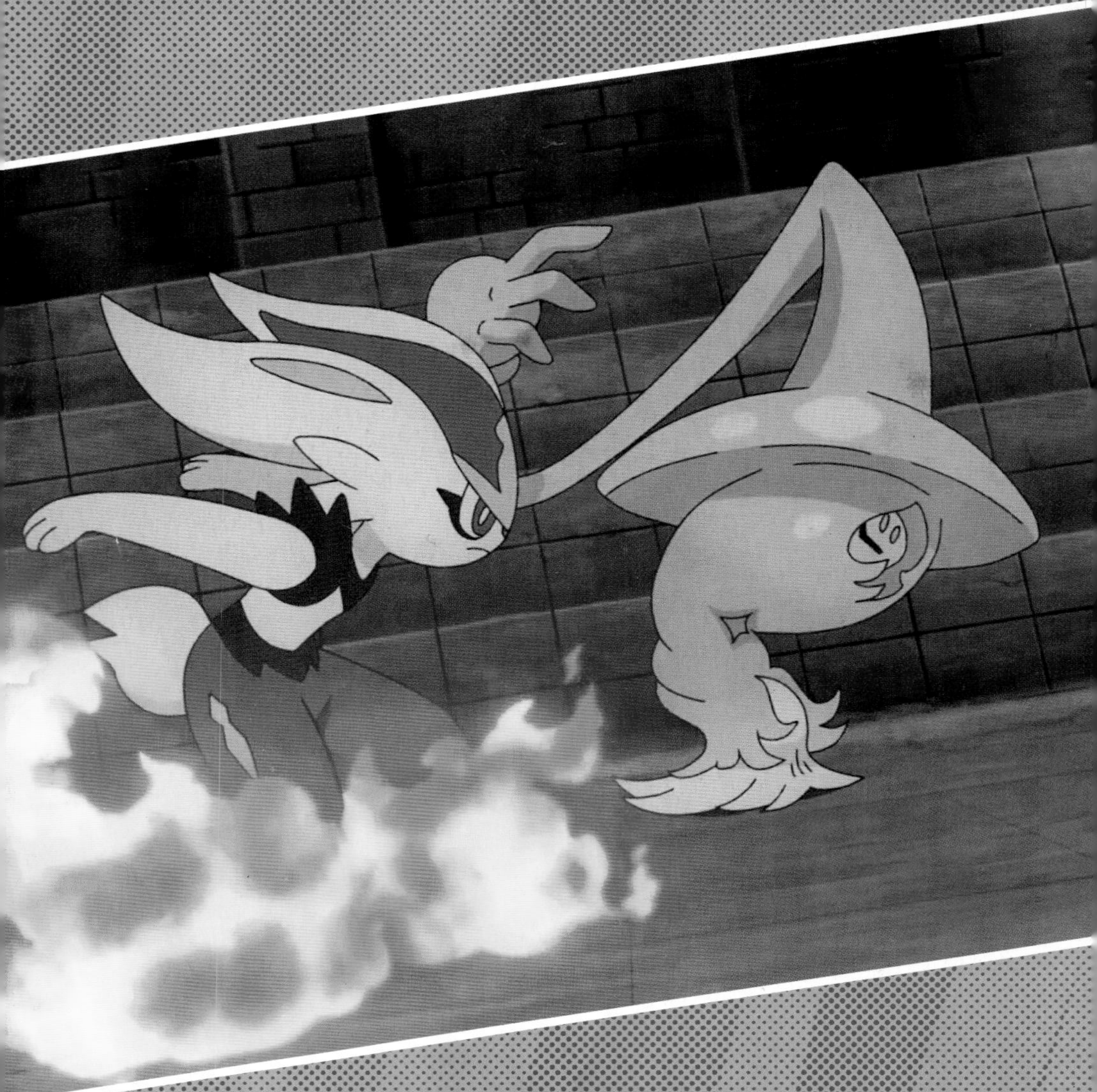

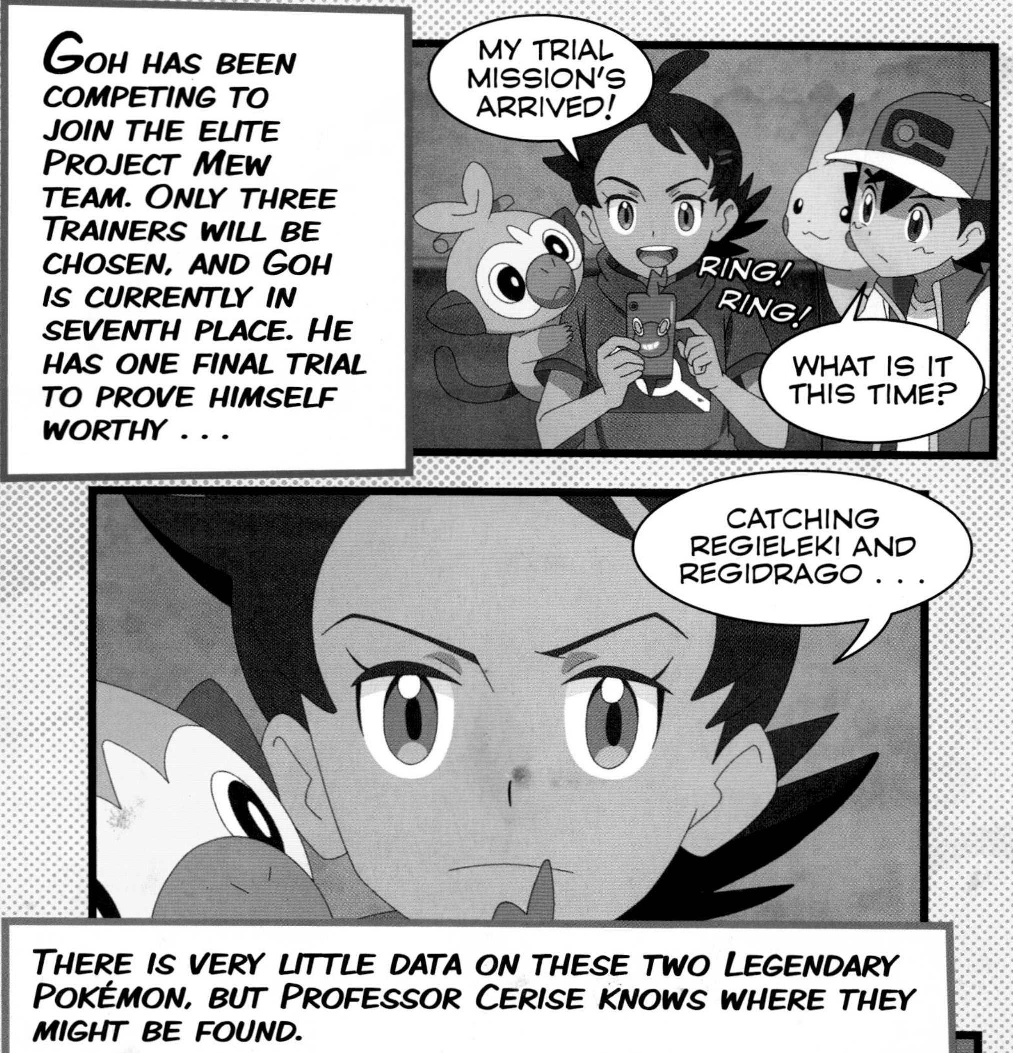
GOH HAS BEEN COMPETING TO JOIN THE ELITE PROJECT MEW TEAM. ONLY THREE TRAINERS WILL BE CHOSEN, AND GOH IS CURRENTLY IN SEVENTH PLACE. HE HAS ONE FINAL TRIAL TO PROVE HIMSELF WORTHY . . .
MY TRIAL MISSION'S ARRIVED!
RING! RING!
WHAT IS IT THIS TIME?
CATCHING REGIELEKI AND REGIDRAGO . . .
THERE IS VERY LITTLE DATA ON THESE TWO LEGENDARY POKÉMON, BUT PROFESSOR CERISE KNOWS WHERE THEY MIGHT BE FOUND.
THEY'RE CONNECTED TO A PLACE IN THE GALAR REGION'S CROWN TUNDRA CALLED THE SPLIT-DECISION RUINS.

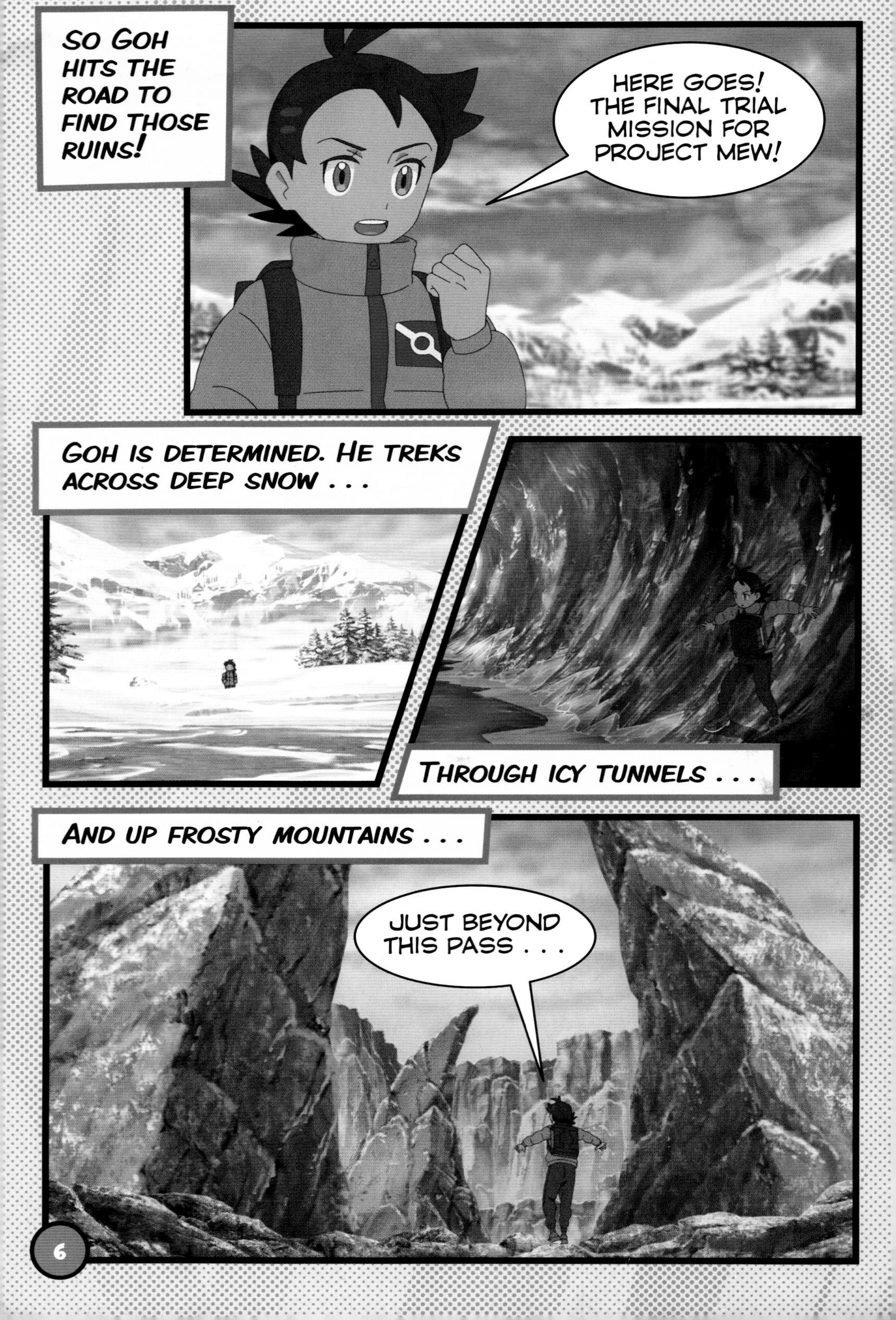
SO GOH HITS THE ROAD TO FIND THOSE RUINS!
HERE GOES! THE FINAL TRIAL MISSION FOR PROJECT MEW!
GOH IS DETERMINED. HE TREKS ACROSS DEEP SNOW . . .
THROUGH ICY TUNNELS . . .
AND UP FROSTY MOUNTAINS . . .
JUST BEYOND THIS PASS . . .

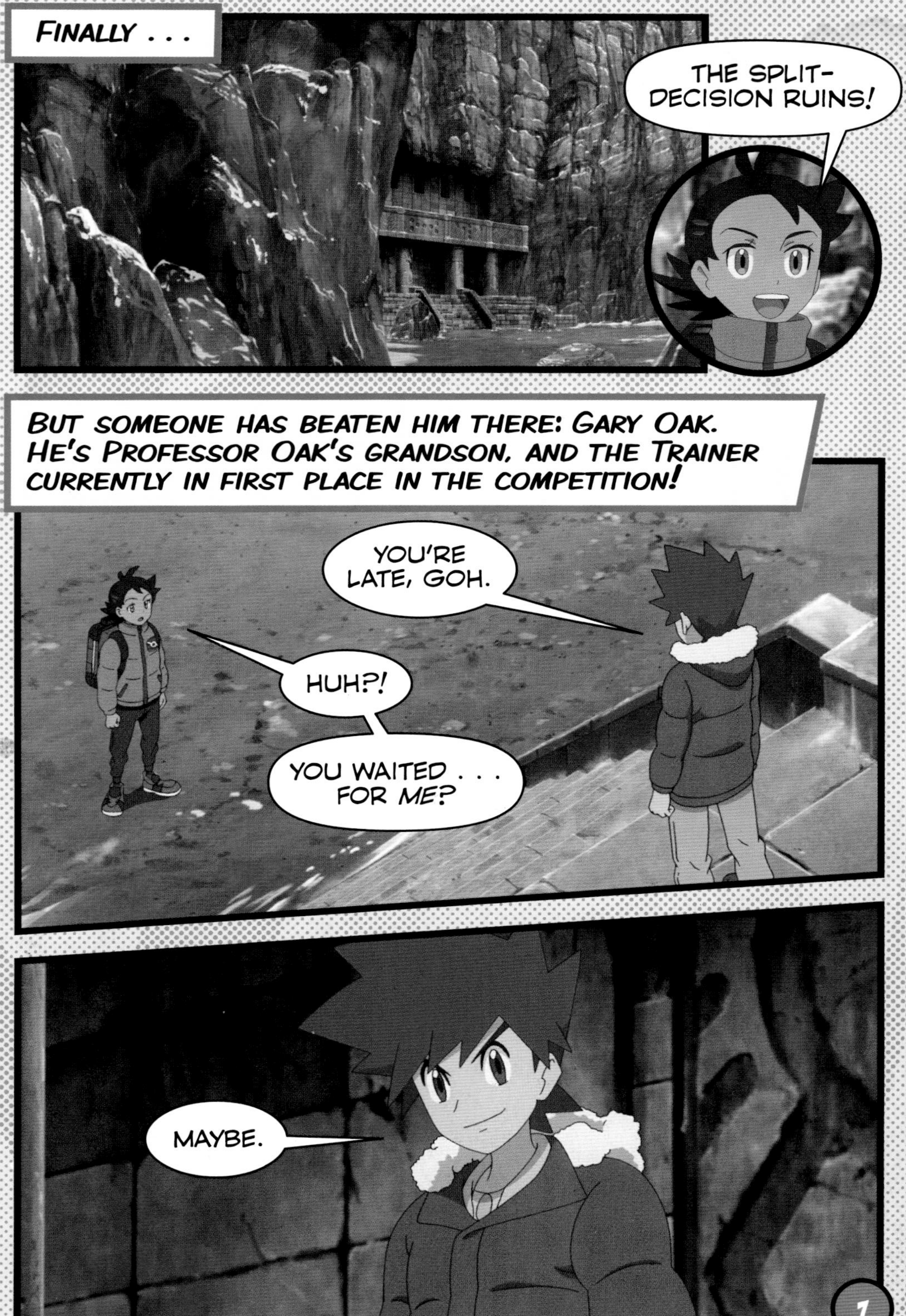
FINALLY . . .
THE SPLIT-DECISION RUINS!
BUT SOMEONE HAS BEATEN HIM THERE: GARY OAK. HE'S PROFESSOR OAK'S GRANDSON, AND THE TRAINER CURRENTLY IN FIRST PLACE IN THE COMPETITION!
YOU'RE LATE, GOH.
HUH?!
YOU WAITED . . . FOR ME?
MAYBE.

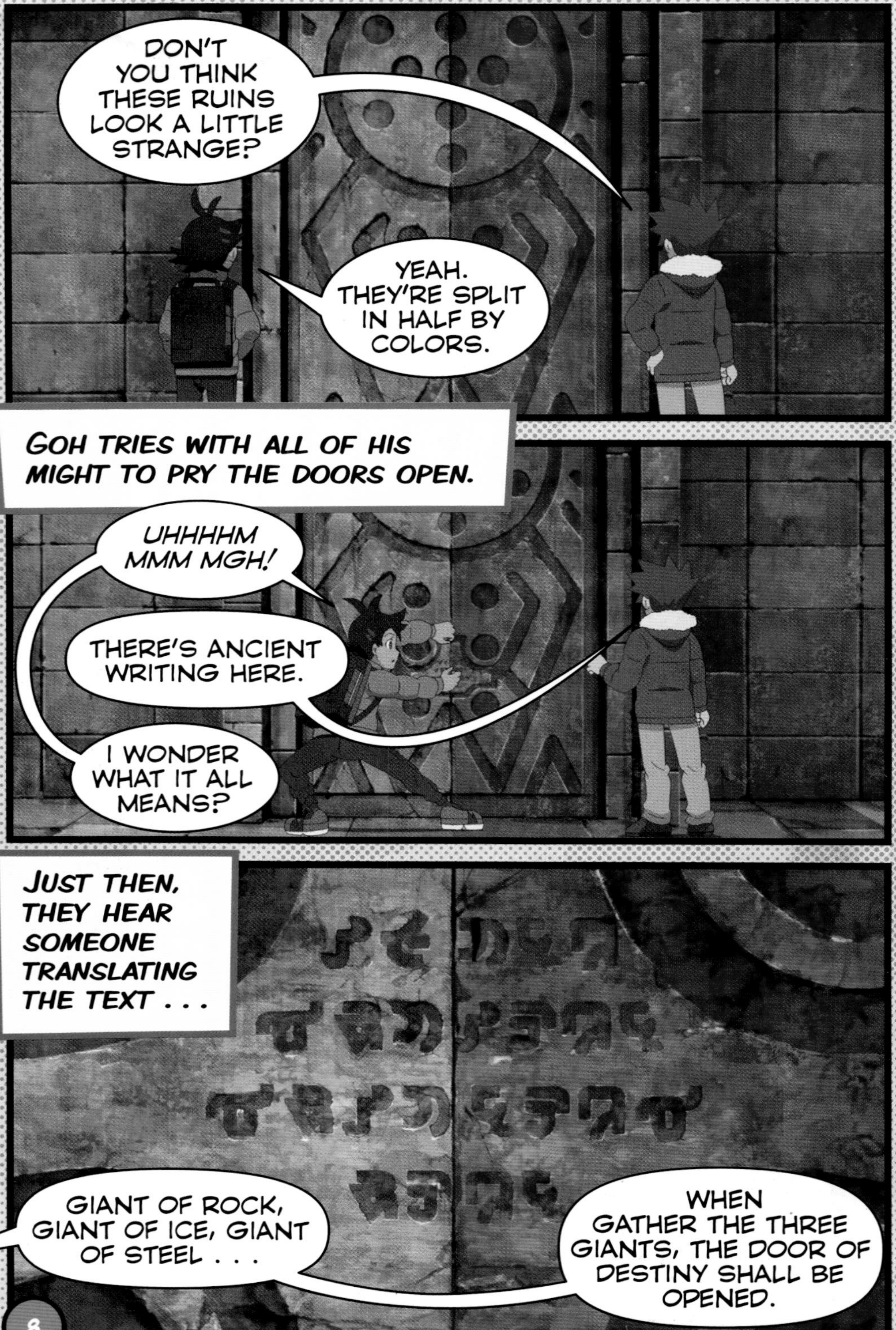
DON'T YOU THINK THESE RUINS LOOK A LITTLE STRANGE?
YEAH. THEY'RE SPLIT IN HALF BY COLORS.
GOH TRIES WITH ALL OF HIS MIGHT TO PRY THE DOORS OPEN.
UHHHHM MMM MGH!
THERE'S ANCIENT WRITING HERE.
I WONDER WHAT IT ALL MEANS?
JUST THEN, THEY HEAR SOMEONE TRANSLATING THE TEXT . . .
GIANT OF ROCK, GIANT OF ICE, GIANT OF STEEL . . .
WHEN GATHER THE THREE GIANTS, THE DOOR OF DESTINY SHALL BE OPENED.

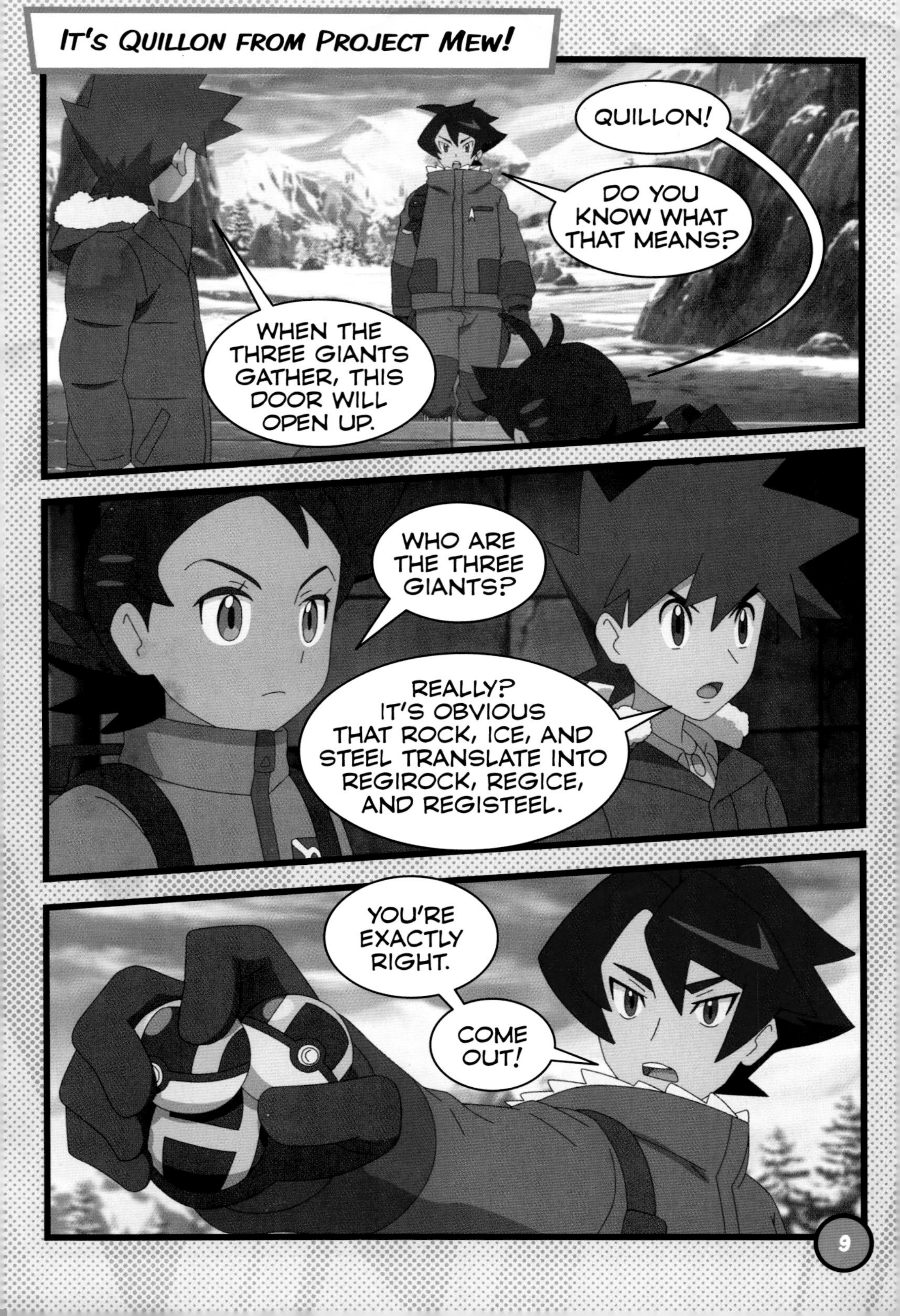
IT'S QUILLON FROM PROJECT MEW!
QUILLON!
DO YOU KNOW WHAT THAT MEANS?
WHEN THE THREE GIANTS GATHER, THIS DOOR WILL OPEN UP.
WHO ARE THE THREE GIANTS?
REALLY? IT'S OBVIOUS THAT ROCK, ICE, AND STEEL TRANSLATE INTO REGIROCK, REGICE, AND REGISTEEL.
YOU'RE EXACTLY RIGHT.
COME OUT!

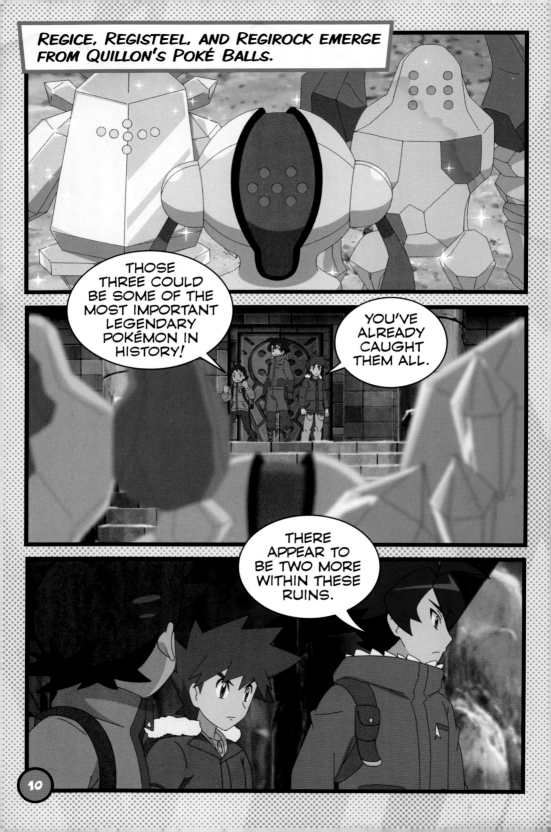

REGICE, REGISTEEL, AND REGIROCK EMERGE FROM QUILLON'S POKÉ BALLS.

THOSE THREE COULD BE SOME OF THE MOST IMPORTANT LEGENDARY POKÉMON IN HISTORY!

YOU'VE ALREADY CAUGHT THEM ALL.

THERE APPEAR TO BE TWO MORE WITHIN THESE RUINS.

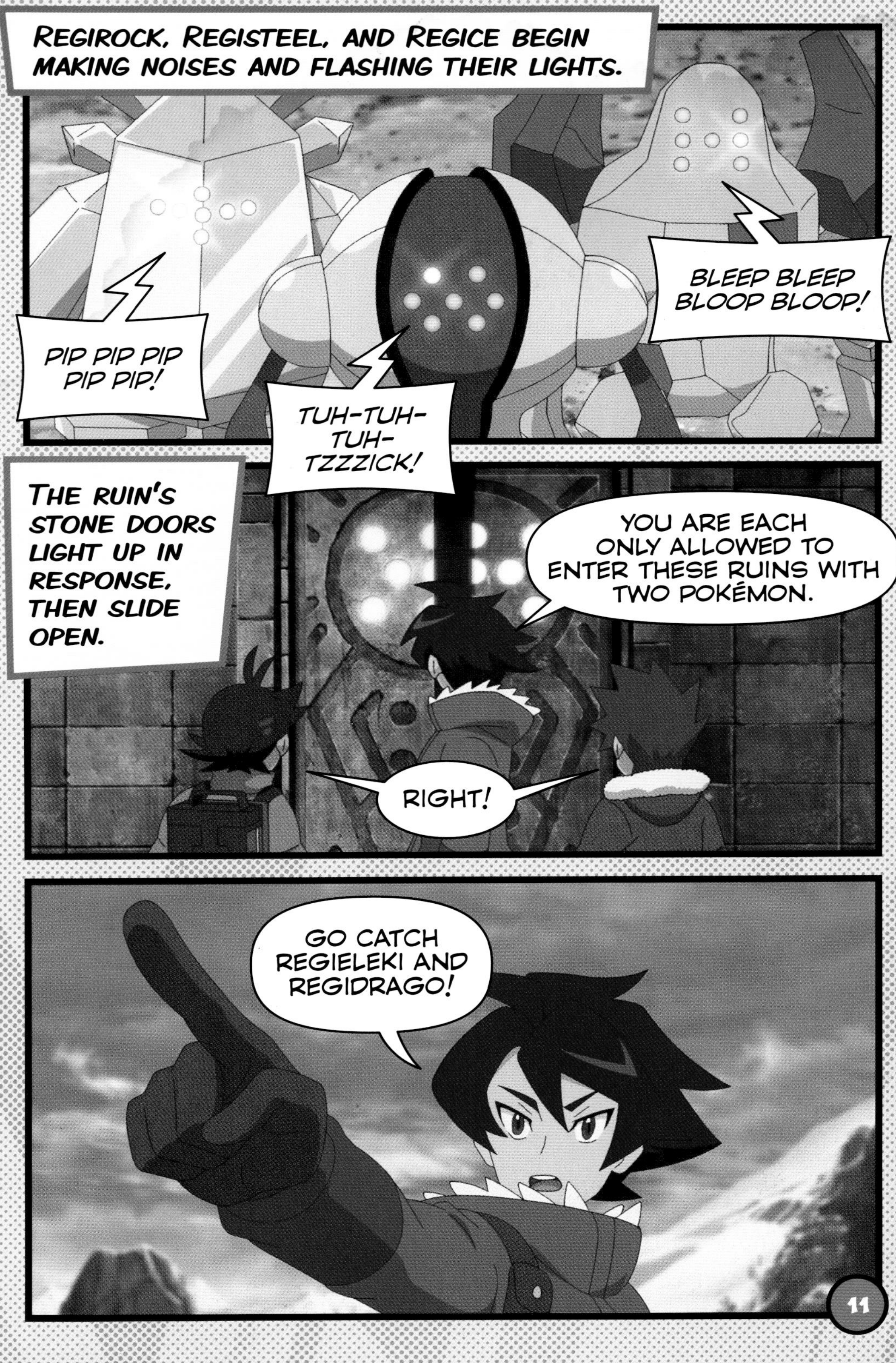
REGIROCK, REGISTEEL, AND REGICE BEGIN MAKING NOISES AND FLASHING THEIR LIGHTS.
PIP PIP PIP PIP PIP!
TUH-TUH-TUH-TZZZICK!
BLEEP BLEEP BLOOP BLOOP!
THE RUIN'S STONE DOORS LIGHT UP IN RESPONSE, THEN SLIDE OPEN.
YOU ARE EACH ONLY ALLOWED TO ENTER THESE RUINS WITH TWO POKÉMON.
RIGHT!
GO CATCH REGIELEKI AND REGIDRAGO!

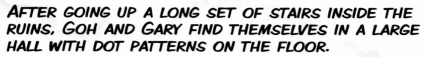

AFTER GOING UP A LONG SET OF STAIRS INSIDE THE RUINS, GOH AND GARY FIND THEMSELVES IN A LARGE HALL WITH DOT PATTERNS ON THE FLOOR.

THERE MUST BE A TRICK TO ALL THIS.

COULD THE PATTERN AT THE ENTRANCE BE A HINT FOR WHAT TO DO NEXT?

IF I STEP ON THE SAME DOTS AS THE PATTERN . . .

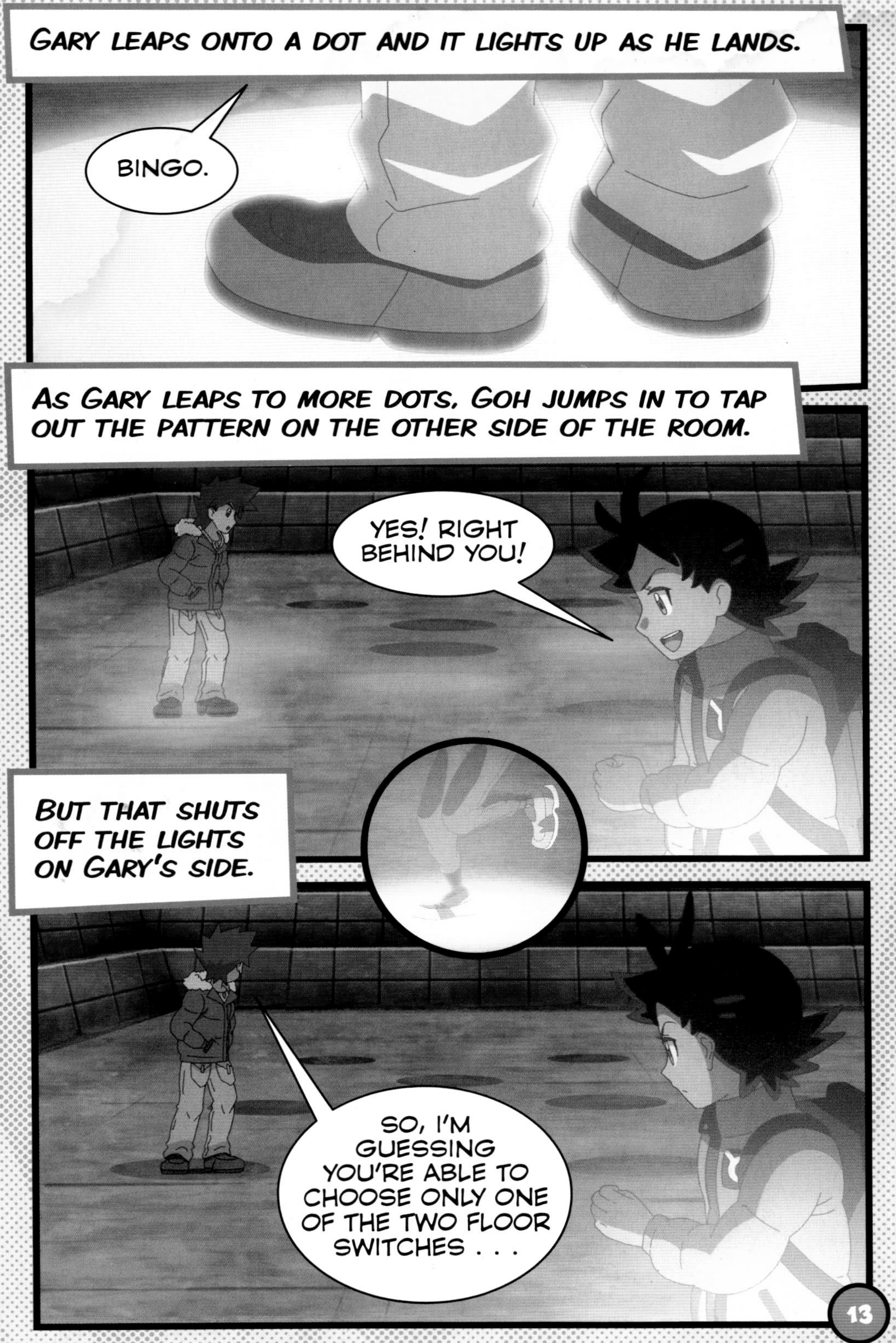
GARY LEAPS ONTO A DOT AND IT LIGHTS UP AS HE LANDS.
BINGO.
AS GARY LEAPS TO MORE DOTS, GOH JUMPS IN TO TAP OUT THE PATTERN ON THE OTHER SIDE OF THE ROOM.
YES! RIGHT BEHIND YOU!
BUT THAT SHUTS OFF THE LIGHTS ON GARY'S SIDE.
SO, I'M GUESSING YOU'RE ABLE TO CHOOSE ONLY ONE OF THE TWO FLOOR SWITCHES . . .

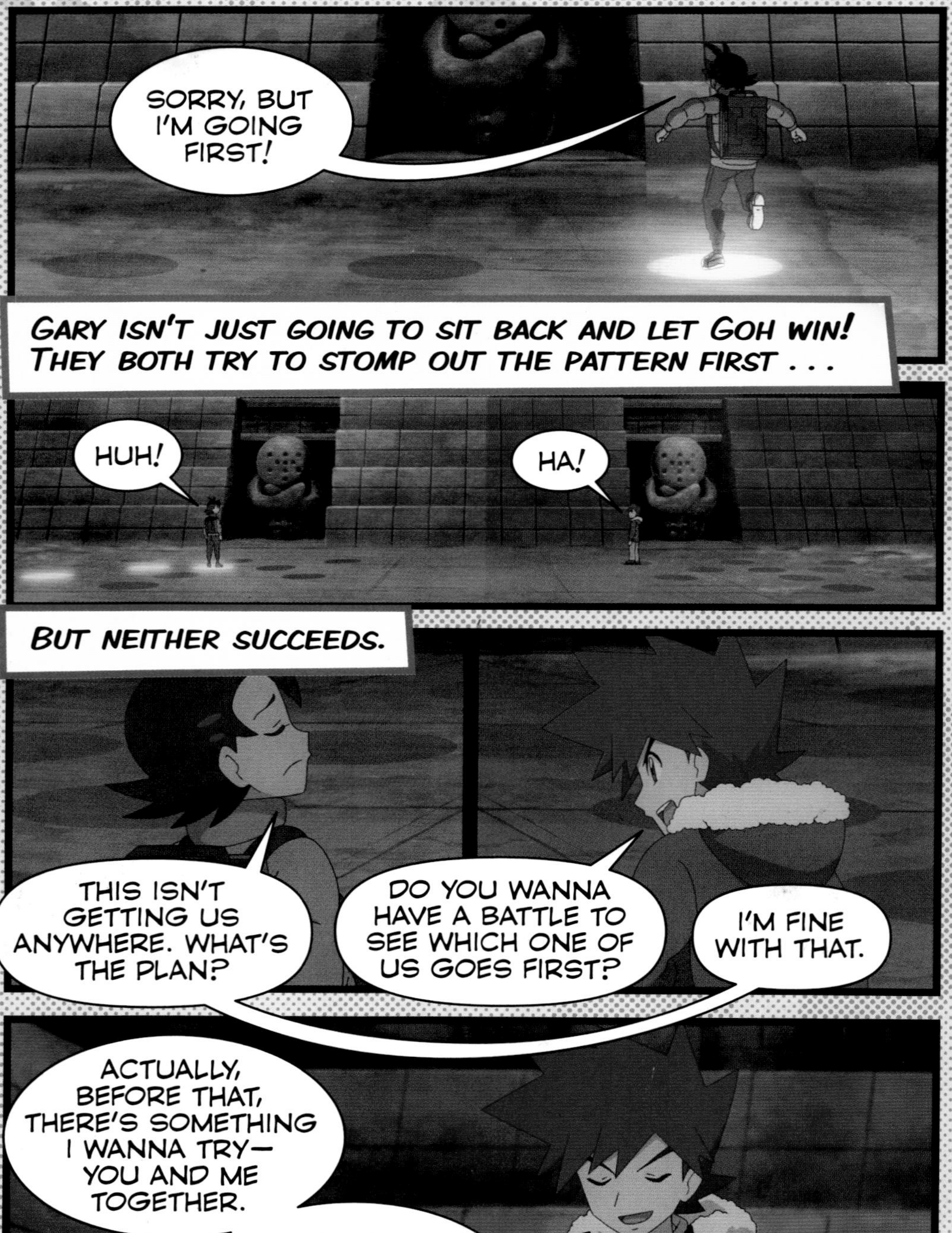
SORRY, BUT I'M GOING FIRST!
GARY ISN'T JUST GOING TO SIT BACK AND LET GOH WIN! THEY BOTH TRY TO STOMP OUT THE PATTERN FIRST . . .
HUH!
HA!
BUT NEITHER SUCCEEDS.
THIS ISN'T GETTING US ANYWHERE. WHAT'S THE PLAN?
DO YOU WANNA HAVE A BATTLE TO SEE WHICH ONE OF US GOES FIRST?
I'M FINE WITH THAT.
ACTUALLY, BEFORE THAT, THERE'S SOMETHING I WANNA TRY— YOU AND ME TOGETHER.
IT'S NOT ABOUT WHO CATCHES THEM BOTH. IT'S HOW WE GET IT DONE!

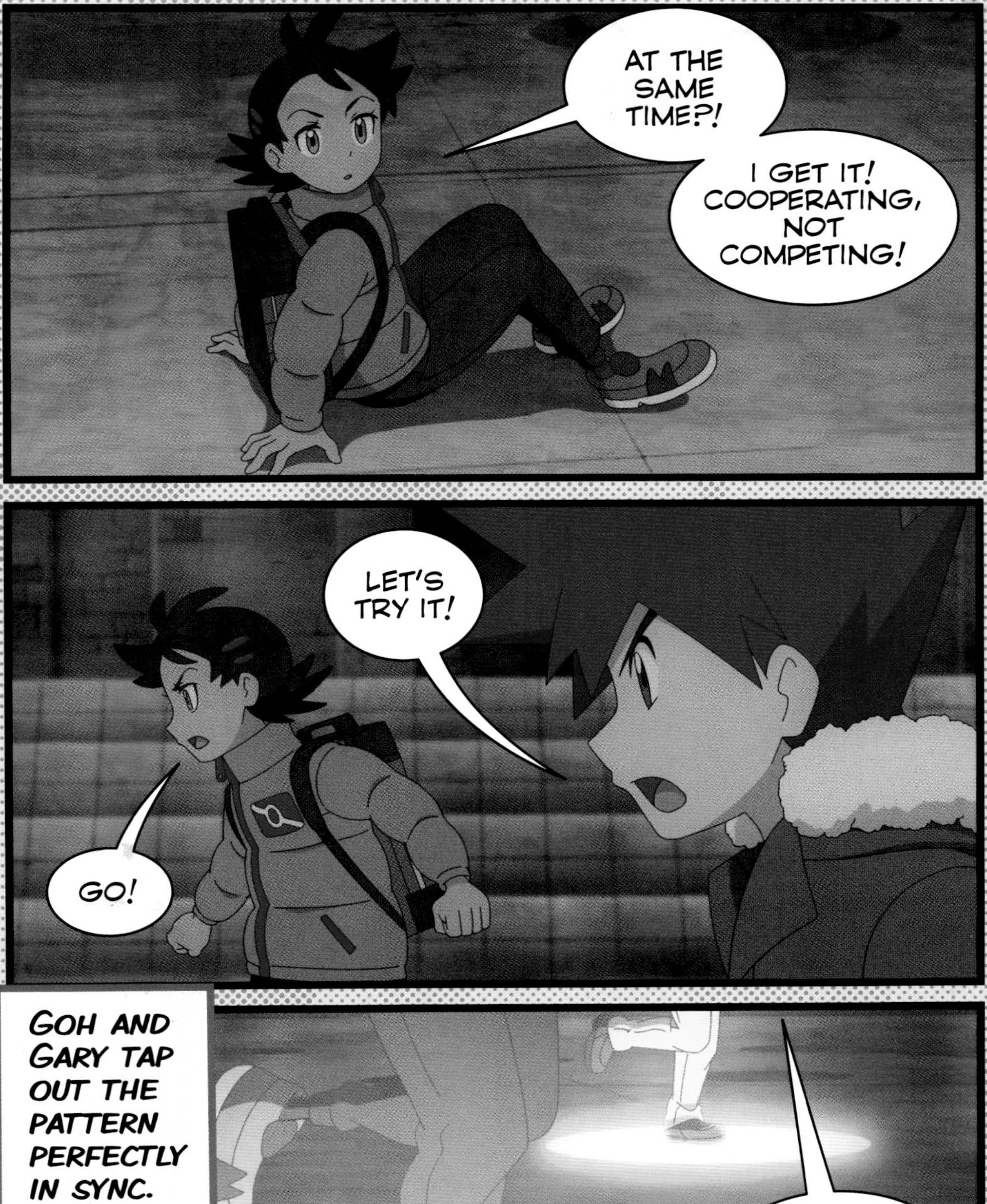
AT THE SAME TIME?!
I GET IT! COOPERATING, NOT COMPETING!
LET'S TRY IT!
GO!
GOH AND GARY TAP OUT THE PATTERN PERFECTLY IN SYNC.
JUST AS PLANNED!

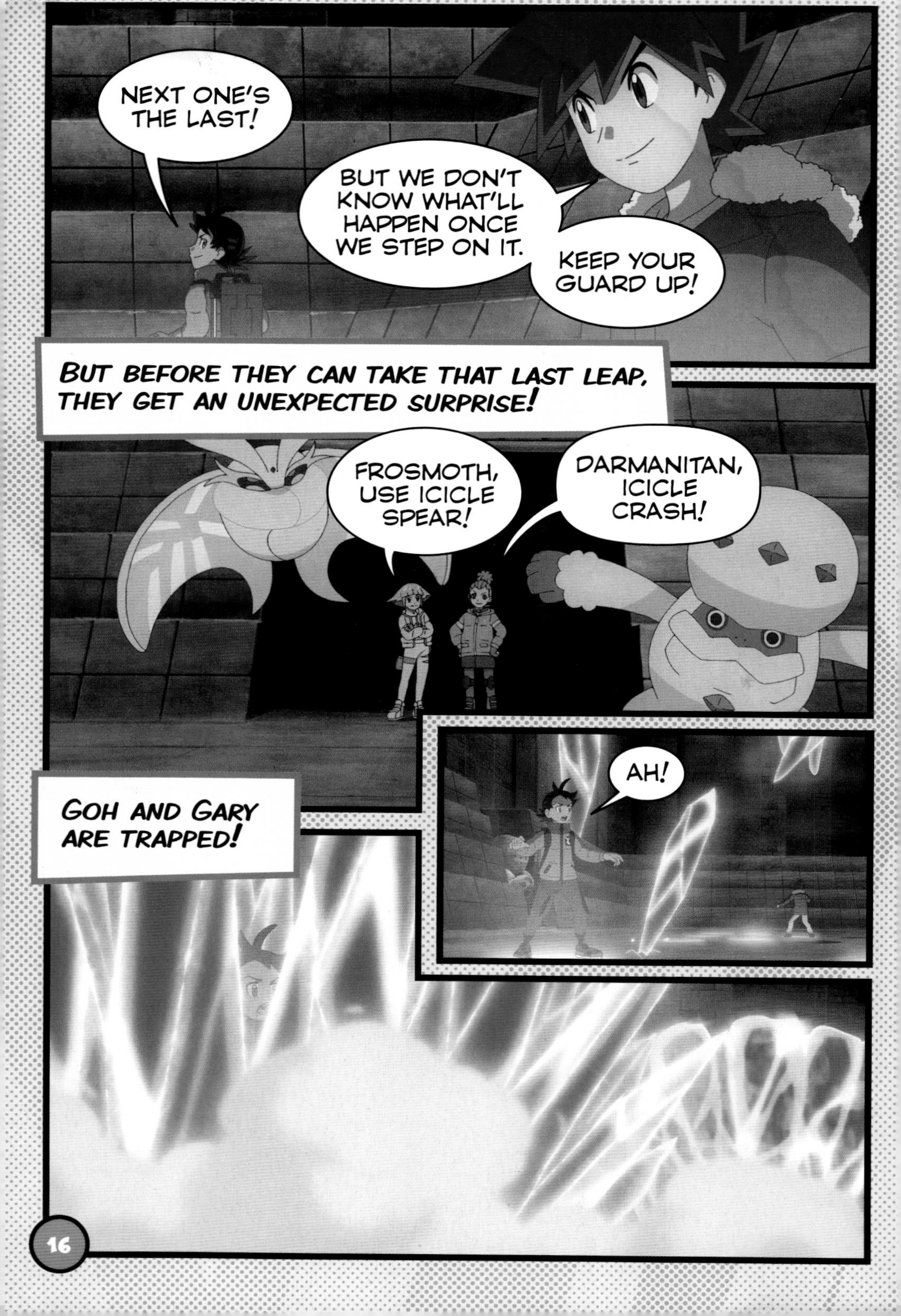
NEXT ONE'S THE LAST!
BUT WE DON'T KNOW WHAT'LL HAPPEN ONCE WE STEP ON IT.
KEEP YOUR GUARD UP!
BUT BEFORE THEY CAN TAKE THAT LAST LEAP, THEY GET AN UNEXPECTED SURPRISE!
FROSMOTH, USE ICICLE SPEAR!
DARMANITAN, ICICLE CRASH!
AH!
GOH AND GARY ARE TRAPPED!

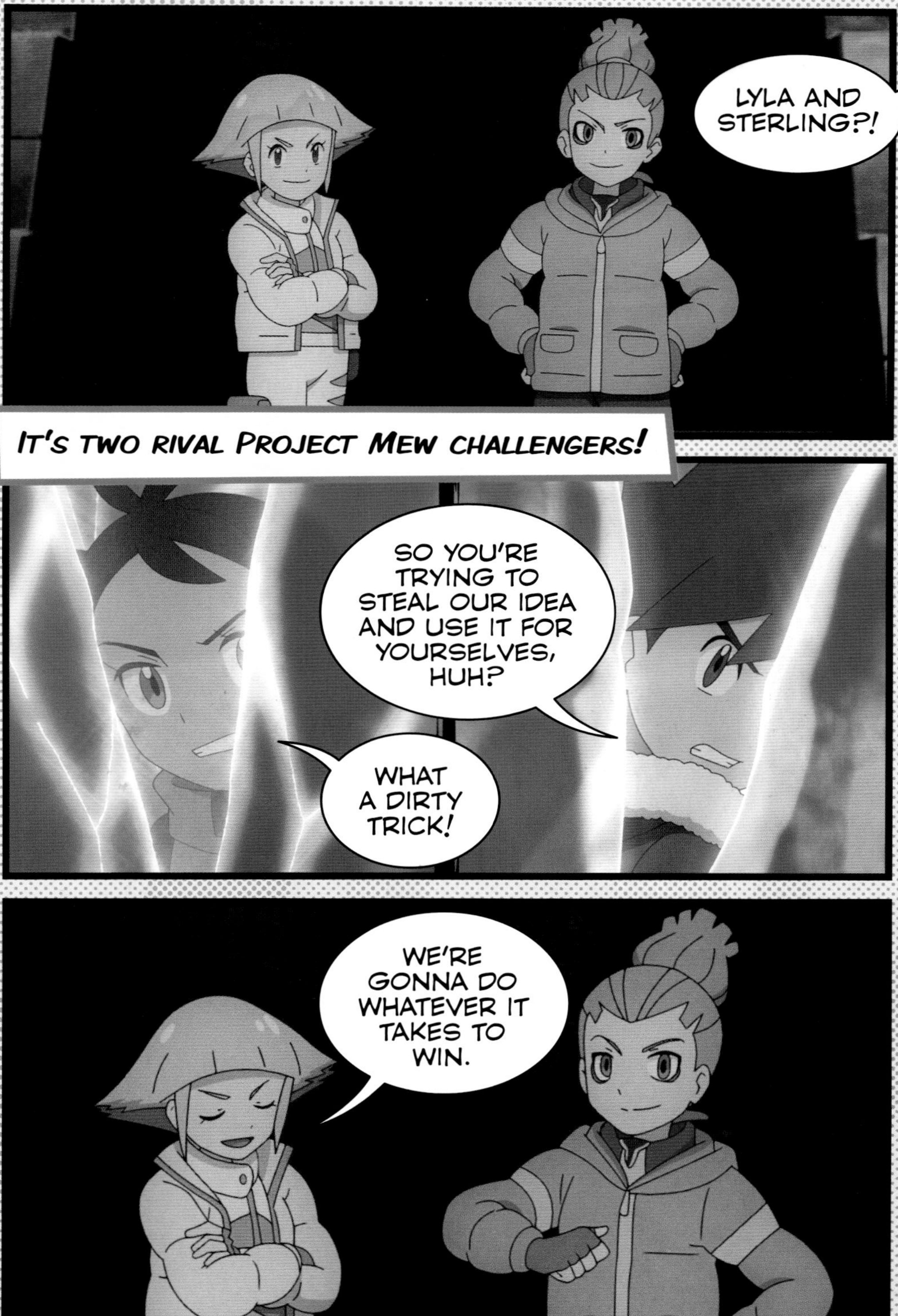

LYLA AND STERLING?!
IT'S TWO RIVAL PROJECT MEW CHALLENGERS!
SO YOU'RE TRYING TO STEAL OUR IDEA AND USE IT FOR YOURSELVES, HUH?
WHAT A DIRTY TRICK!
WE'RE GONNA DO WHATEVER IT TAKES TO WIN.

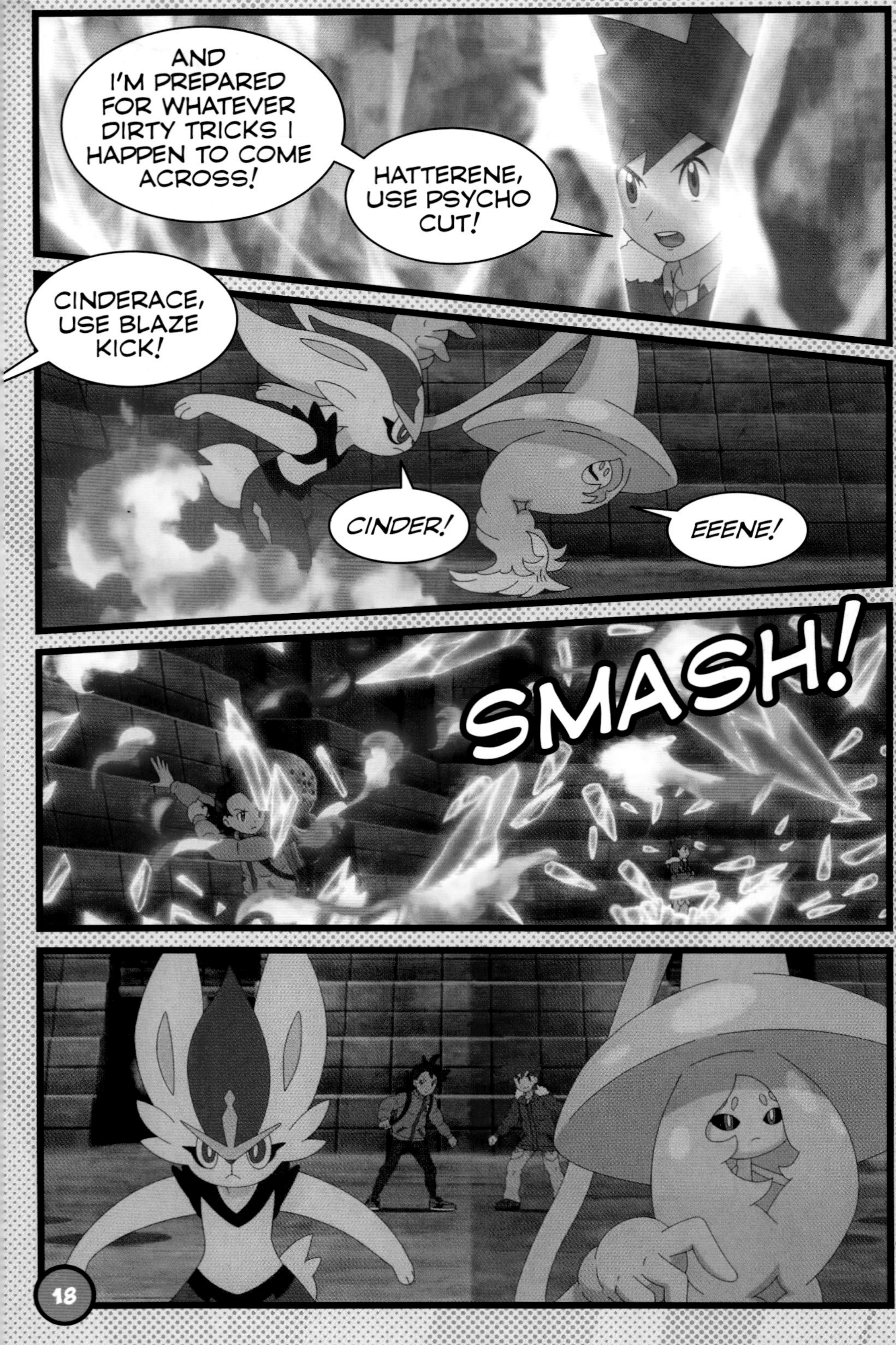
AND I'M PREPARED FOR WHATEVER DIRTY TRICKS I HAPPEN TO COME ACROSS!
HATTERENE, USE PSYCHO CUT!
CINDERACE, USE BLAZE KICK!
CINDER!
EEENE!
SMASH!

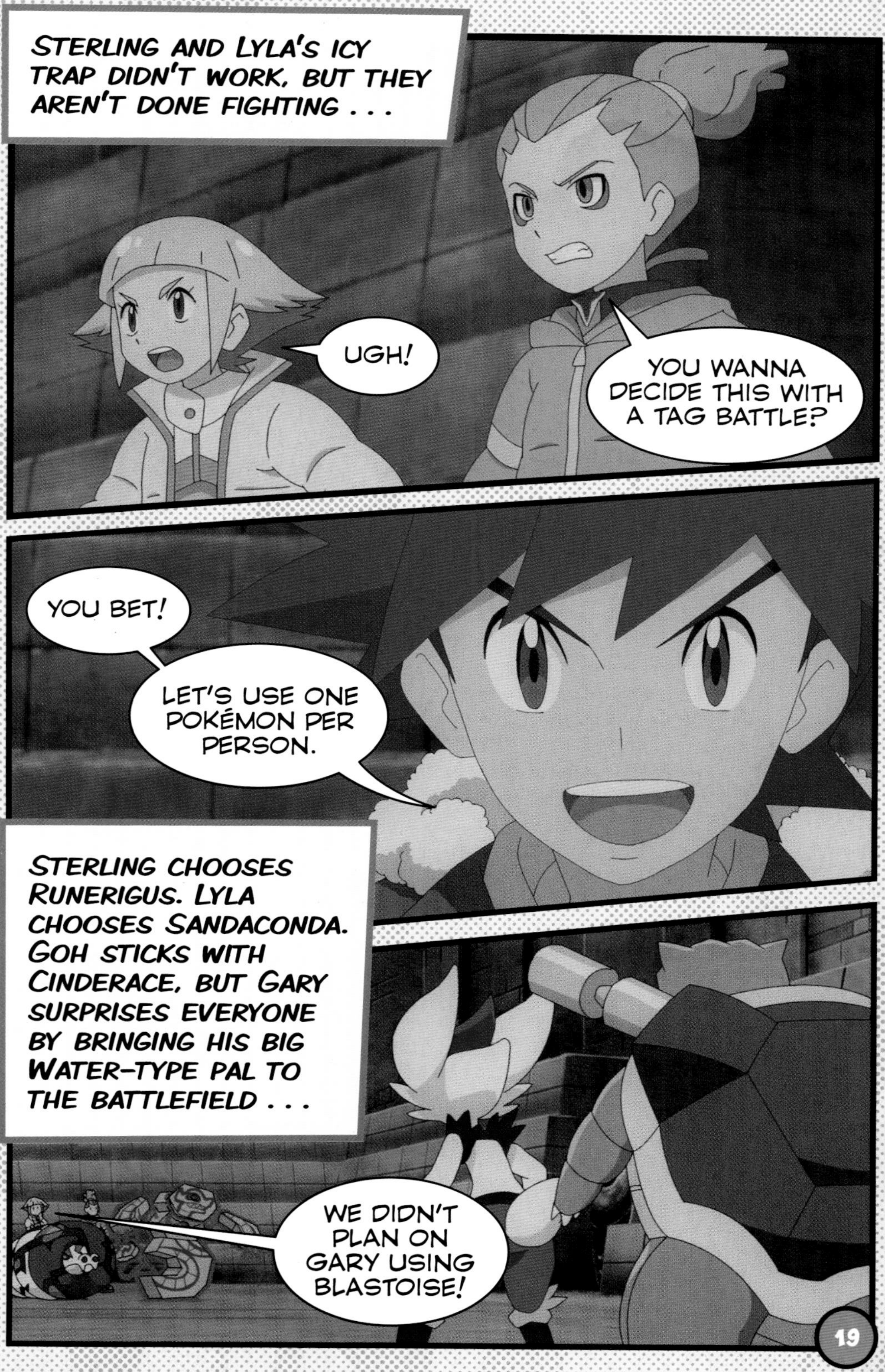
STERLING AND LYLA'S ICY TRAP DIDN'T WORK, BUT THEY AREN'T DONE FIGHTING . . .
UGH!
YOU WANNA DECIDE THIS WITH A TAG BATTLE?
YOU BET!
LET'S USE ONE POKÉMON PER PERSON.
STERLING CHOOSES RUNERIGUS. LYLA CHOOSES SANDACONDA. GOH STICKS WITH CINDERACE, BUT GARY SURPRISES EVERYONE BY BRINGING HIS BIG WATER-TYPE PAL TO THE BATTLEFIELD . . .
WE DIDN'T PLAN ON GARY USING BLASTOISE!

GARY'S GOT STRATEGY, SO LYLA AND STERLING TRY TO USE SPEED TO THEIR ADVANTAGE . . .

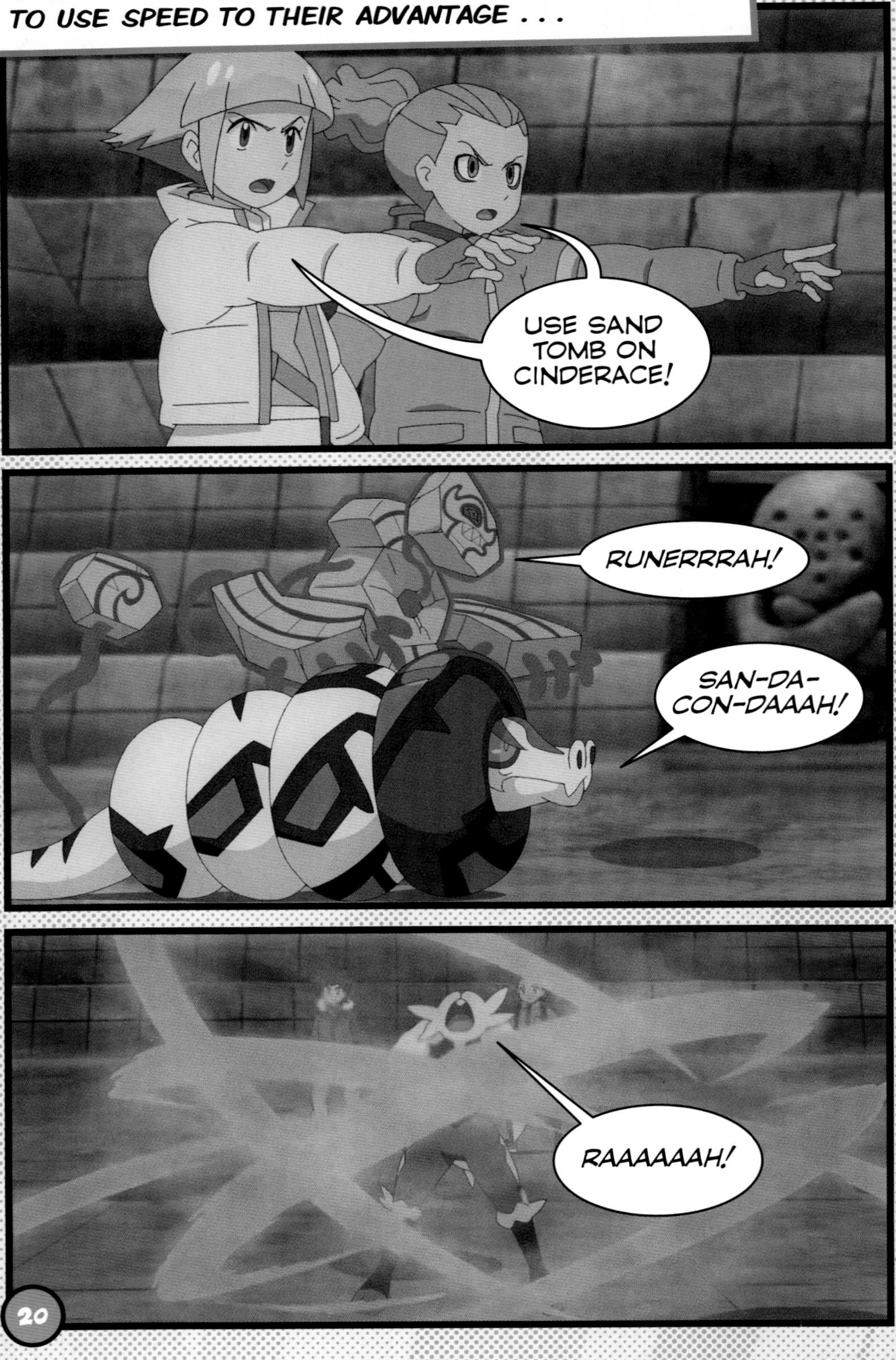
USE SAND TOMB ON CINDERACE!
RUNERRRAH!
SAN-DA-CON-DAAAH!
RAAAAAAH!

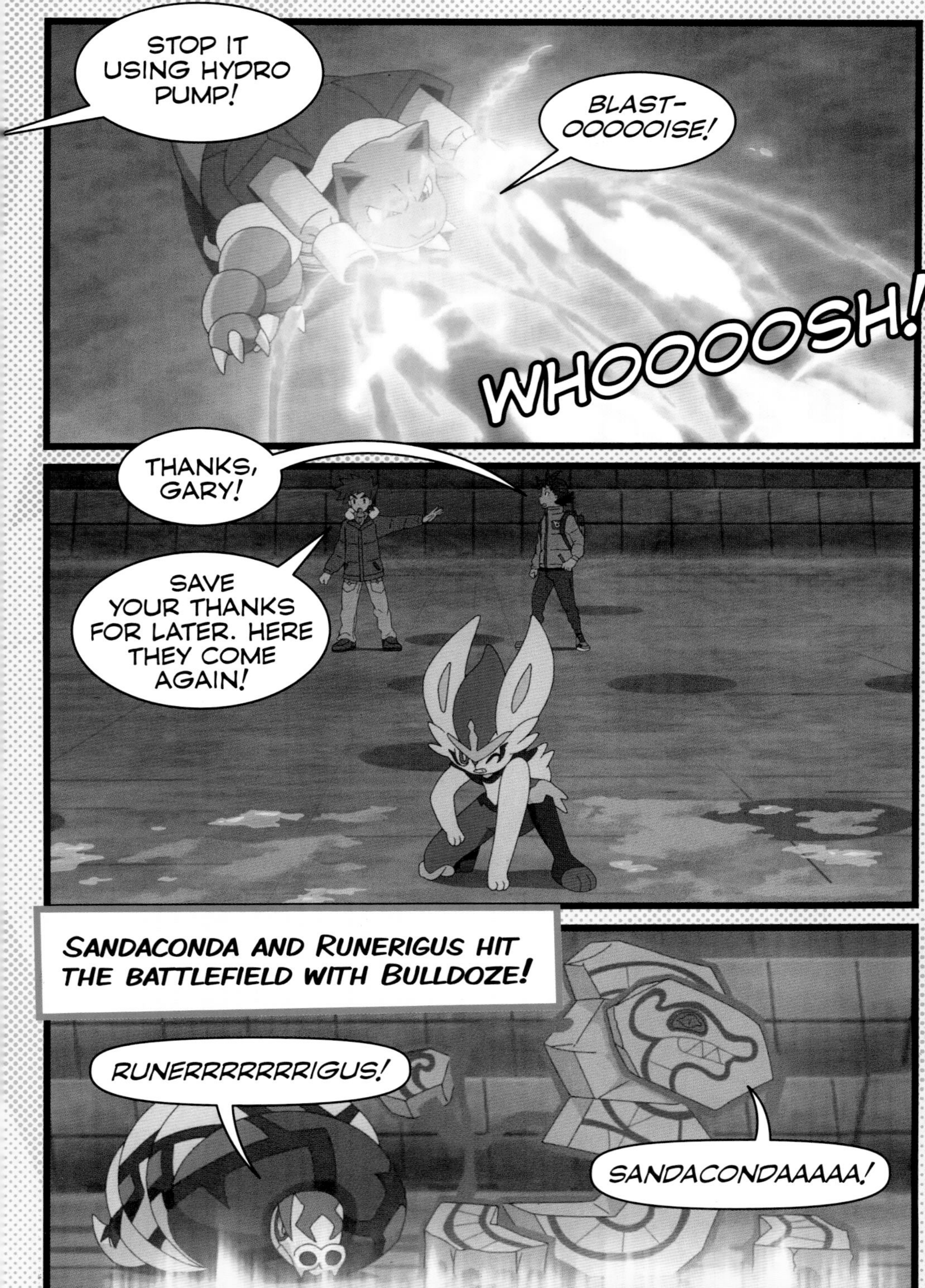
STOP IT USING HYDRO PUMP!
BLAST-OOOOOOISE!
WHOOOOOSH!
THANKS, GARY!
SAVE YOUR THANKS FOR LATER. HERE THEY COME AGAIN!
SANDACONDA AND RUNERIGUS HIT THE BATTLEFIELD WITH BULLDOZE!
RUNERRRRRRRIGUS!
SANDACONDAAAAAA!

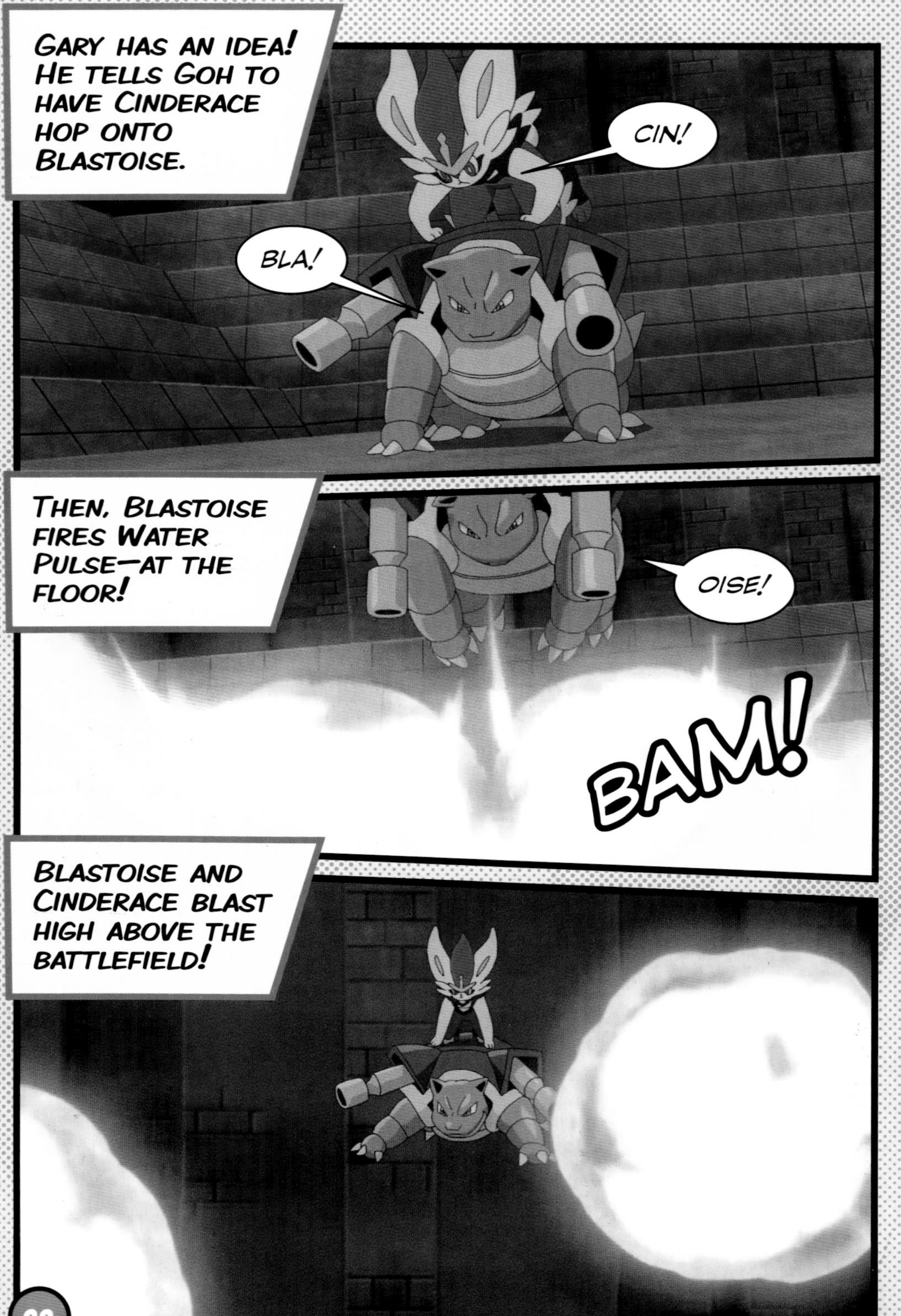
GARY HAS AN IDEA! HE TELLS GOH TO HAVE CINDERACE HOP ONTO BLASTOISE.
CIN!
BLA!
THEN, BLASTOISE FIRES WATER PULSE—AT THE FLOOR!
OISE!
BAM!
BLASTOISE AND CINDERACE BLAST HIGH ABOVE THE BATTLEFIELD!

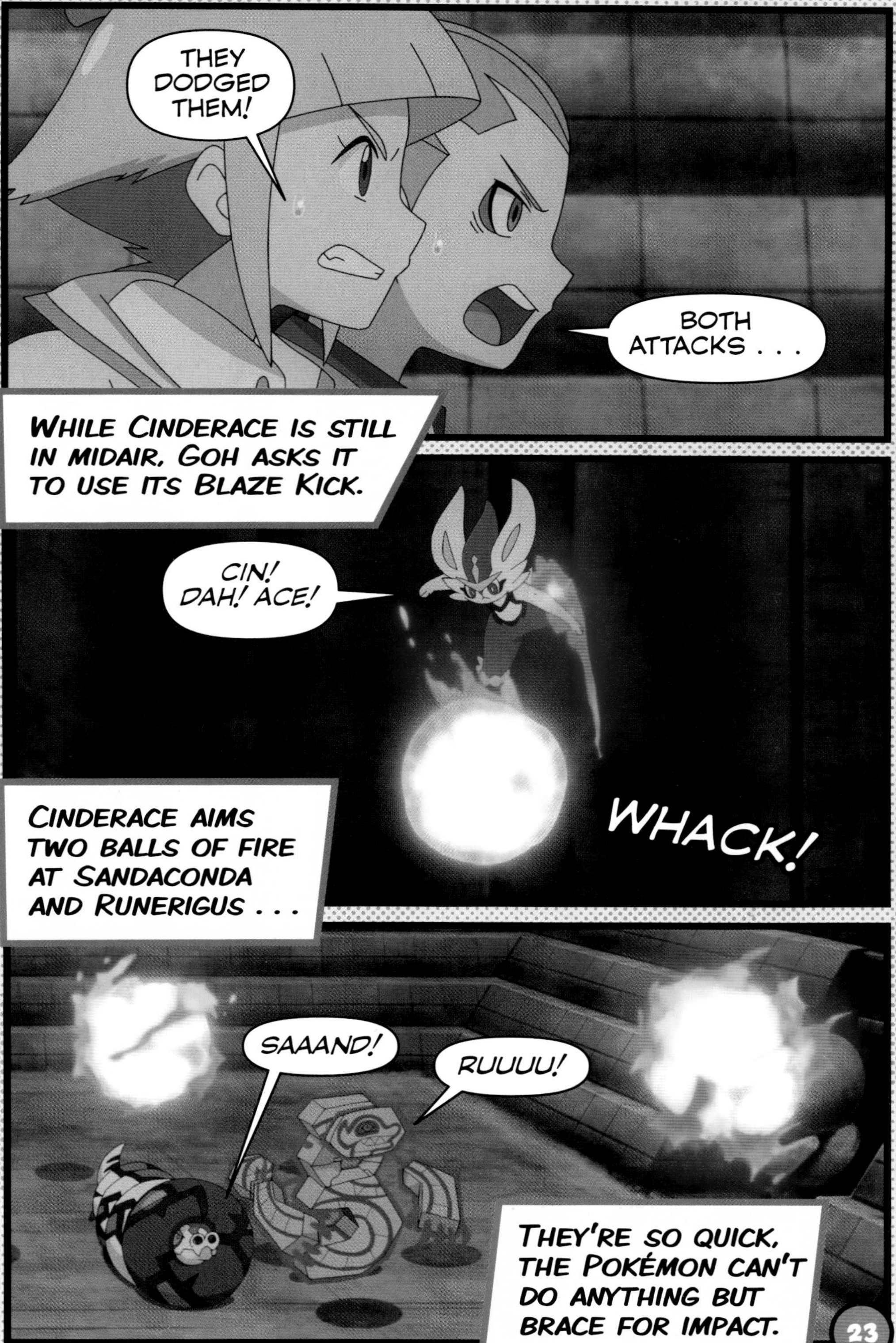
THEY DODGED THEM!
BOTH ATTACKS . . .
WHILE CINDERACE IS STILL IN MIDAIR, GOH ASKS IT TO USE ITS BLAZE KICK.
CIN! DAH! ACE!
WHACK!
CINDERACE AIMS TWO BALLS OF FIRE AT SANDACONDA AND RUNERIGUS . . .
SAAAND!
RUUUU!
THEY'RE SO QUICK, THE POKÉMON CAN'T DO ANYTHING BUT BRACE FOR IMPACT.

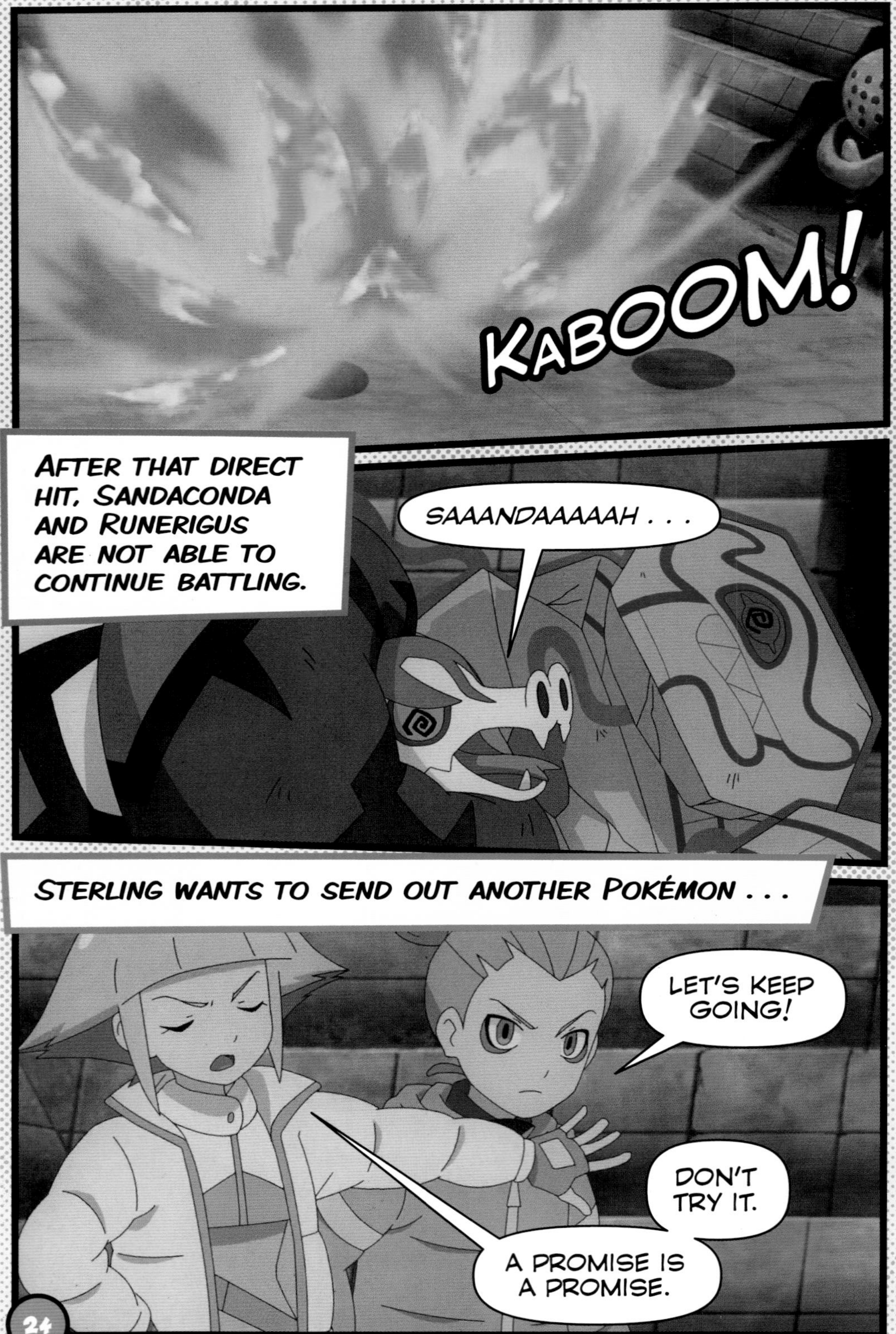
KABOOM!
AFTER THAT DIRECT HIT, SANDACONDA AND RUNERIGUS ARE NOT ABLE TO CONTINUE BATTLING.
SAAANDAAAAAH . . .
STERLING WANTS TO SEND OUT ANOTHER POKÉMON . . .
LET'S KEEP GOING!
DON'T TRY IT.
A PROMISE IS A PROMISE.

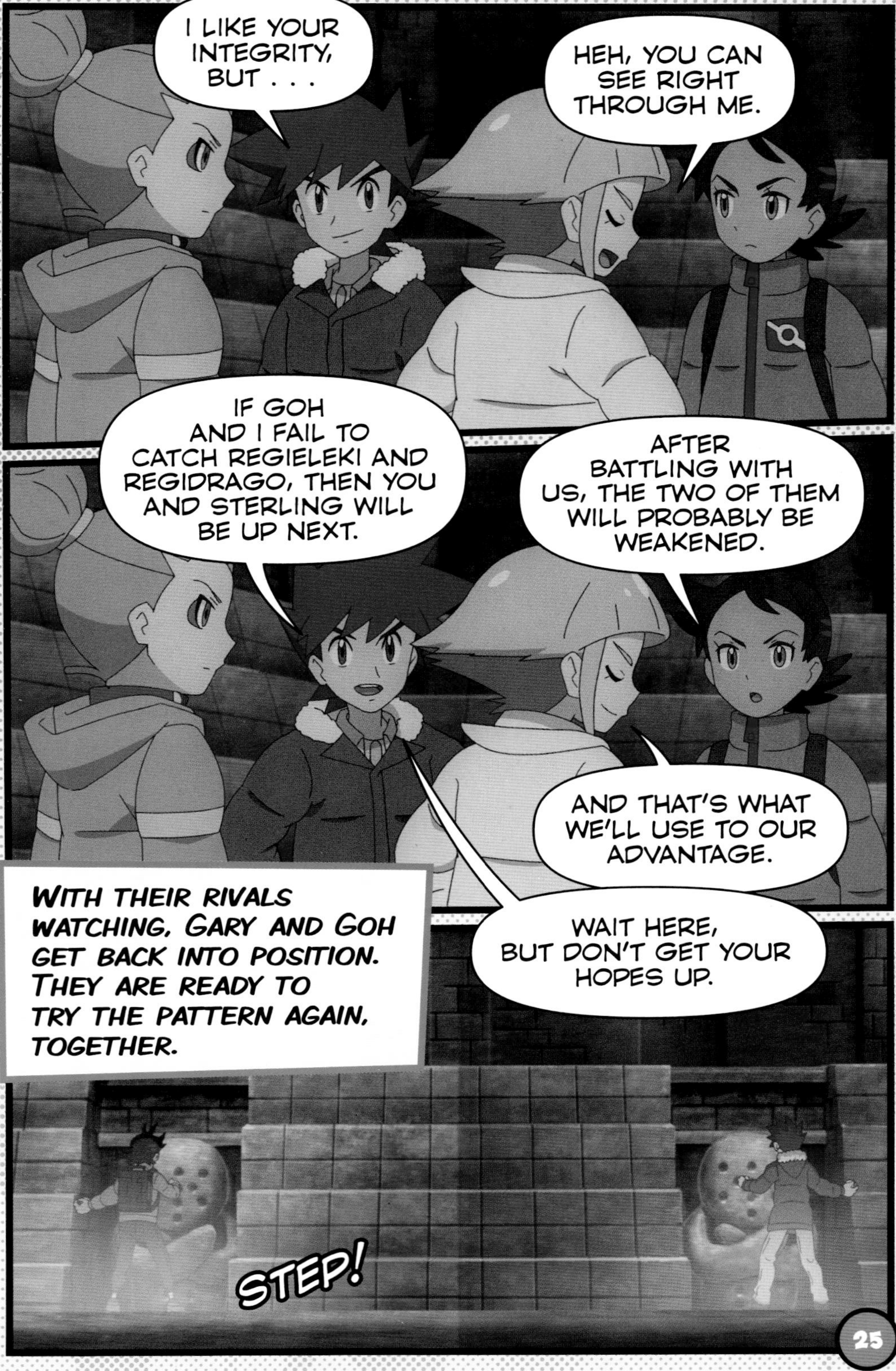
I LIKE YOUR INTEGRITY, BUT . . .
HEH, YOU CAN SEE RIGHT THROUGH ME.
IF GOH AND I FAIL TO CATCH REGIELEKI AND REGIDRAGO, THEN YOU AND STERLING WILL BE UP NEXT.
AFTER BATTLING WITH US, THE TWO OF THEM WILL PROBABLY BE WEAKENED.
AND THAT'S WHAT WE'LL USE TO OUR ADVANTAGE.
WAIT HERE, BUT DON'T GET YOUR HOPES UP.
WITH THEIR RIVALS WATCHING, GARY AND GOH GET BACK INTO POSITION. THEY ARE READY TO TRY THE PATTERN AGAIN, TOGETHER.
STEP!

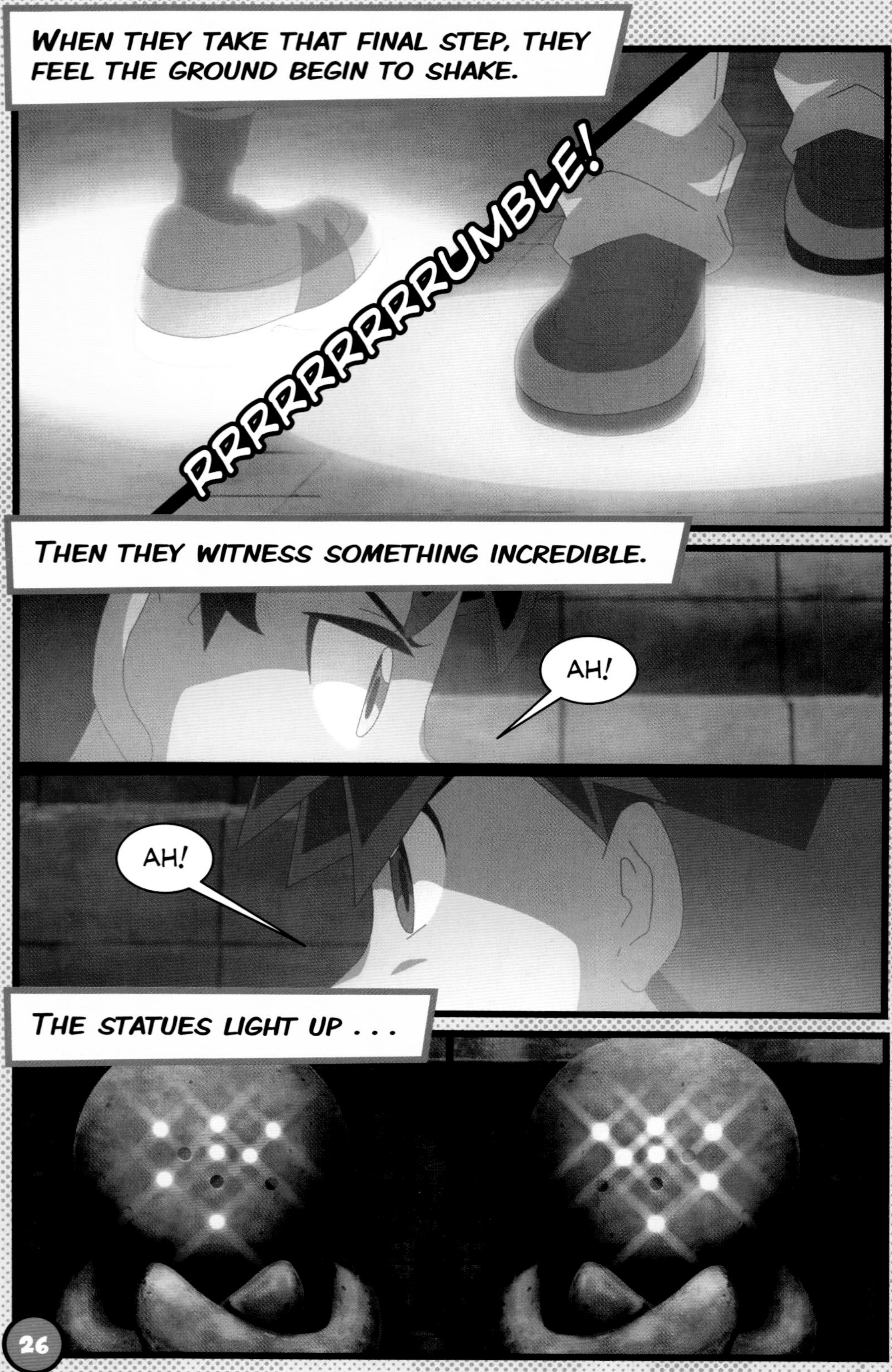
WHEN THEY TAKE THAT FINAL STEP, THEY FEEL THE GROUND BEGIN TO SHAKE.
RRRRRRRRRUMBLE!
THEN THEY WITNESS SOMETHING INCREDIBLE.
AH!
AH!
THE STATUES LIGHT UP . . .

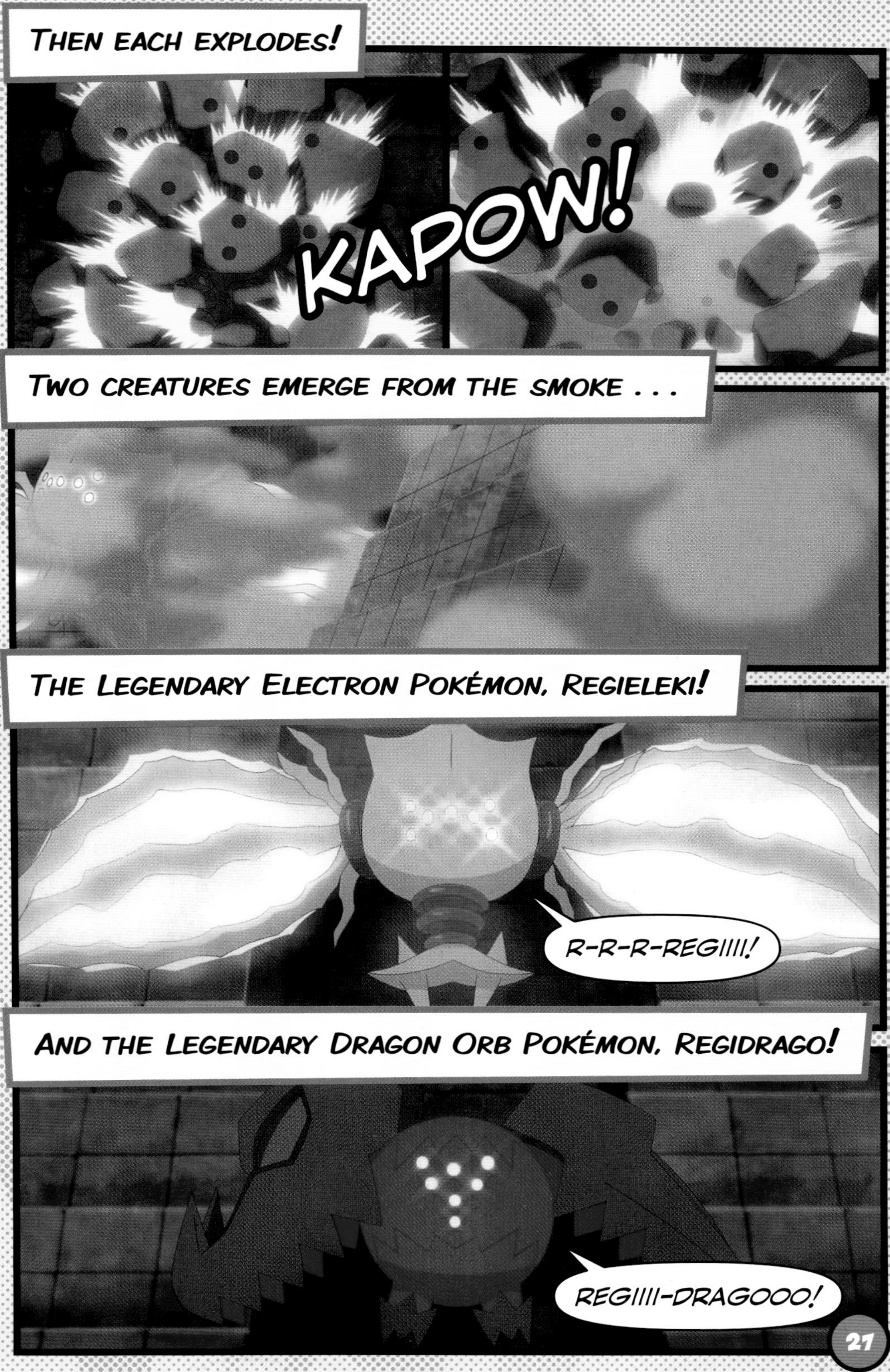

Then each explodes!
KAPOW!
Two creatures emerge from the smoke . . .
The Legendary Electron Pokémon, Regieleki!
R-R-R-REGIIII!
And the Legendary Dragon Orb Pokémon, Regidrago!
REGIIII-DRAGOOO!

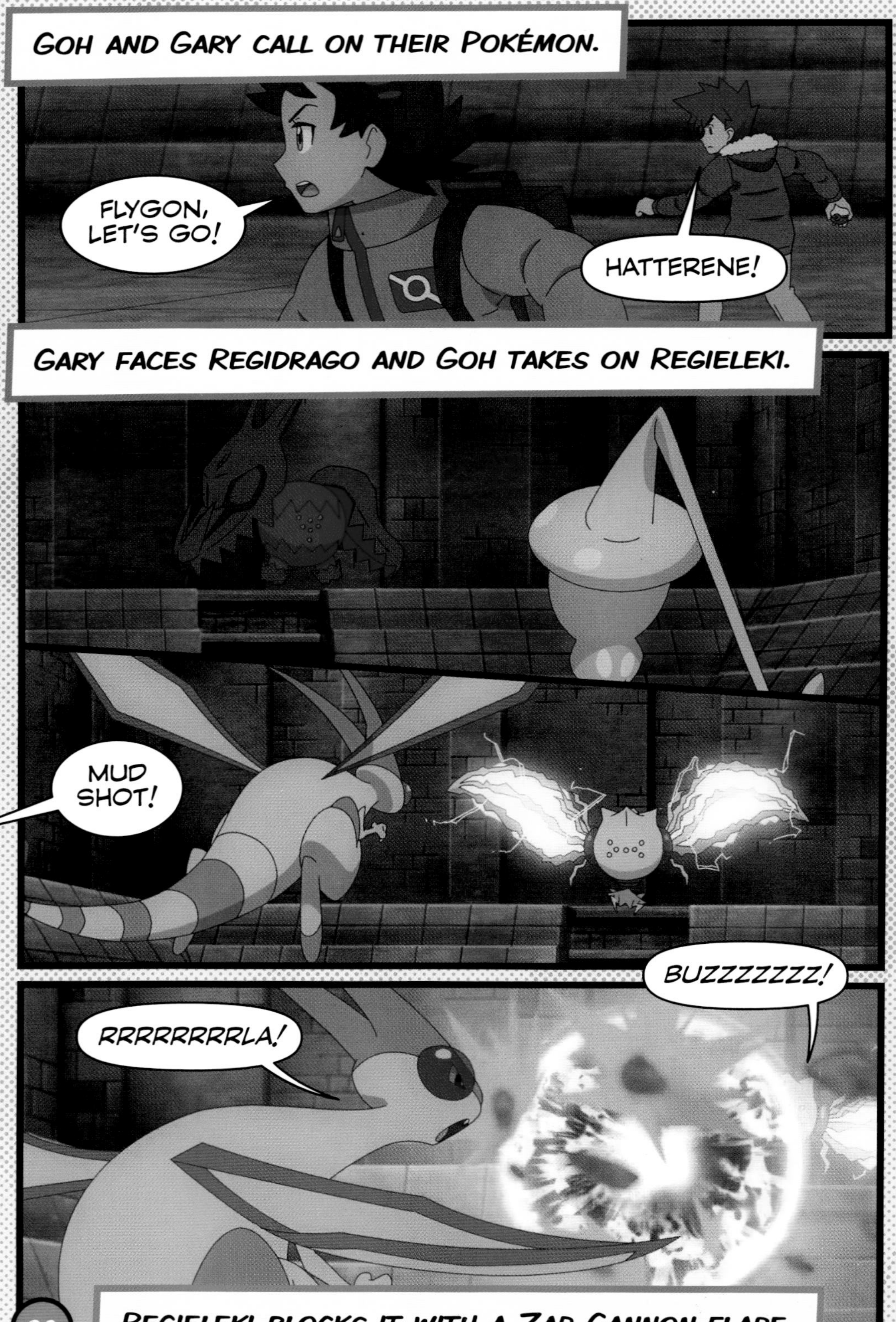
Goh and Gary call on their Pokémon.
FLYGON, LET'S GO!
HATTERENE!
Gary faces Regidrago and Goh takes on Regieleki.
MUD SHOT!
BUZZZZZZZ!
RRRRRRRRLA!
Regieleki blocks it with a Zap Cannon flare.

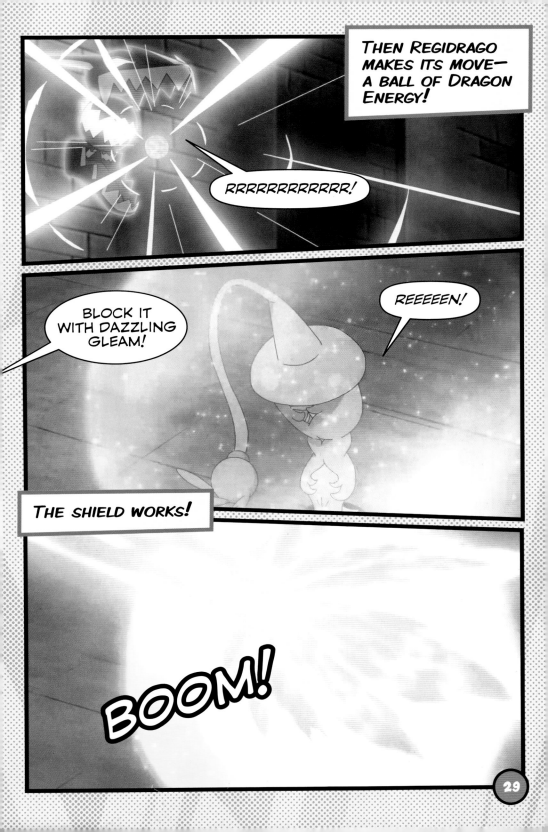

THEN REGIDRAGO MAKES ITS MOVE— A BALL OF DRAGON ENERGY!

RRRRRRRRRRR!

BLOCK IT WITH DAZZLING GLEAM!

REEEEEN!

THE SHIELD WORKS!

BOOM!

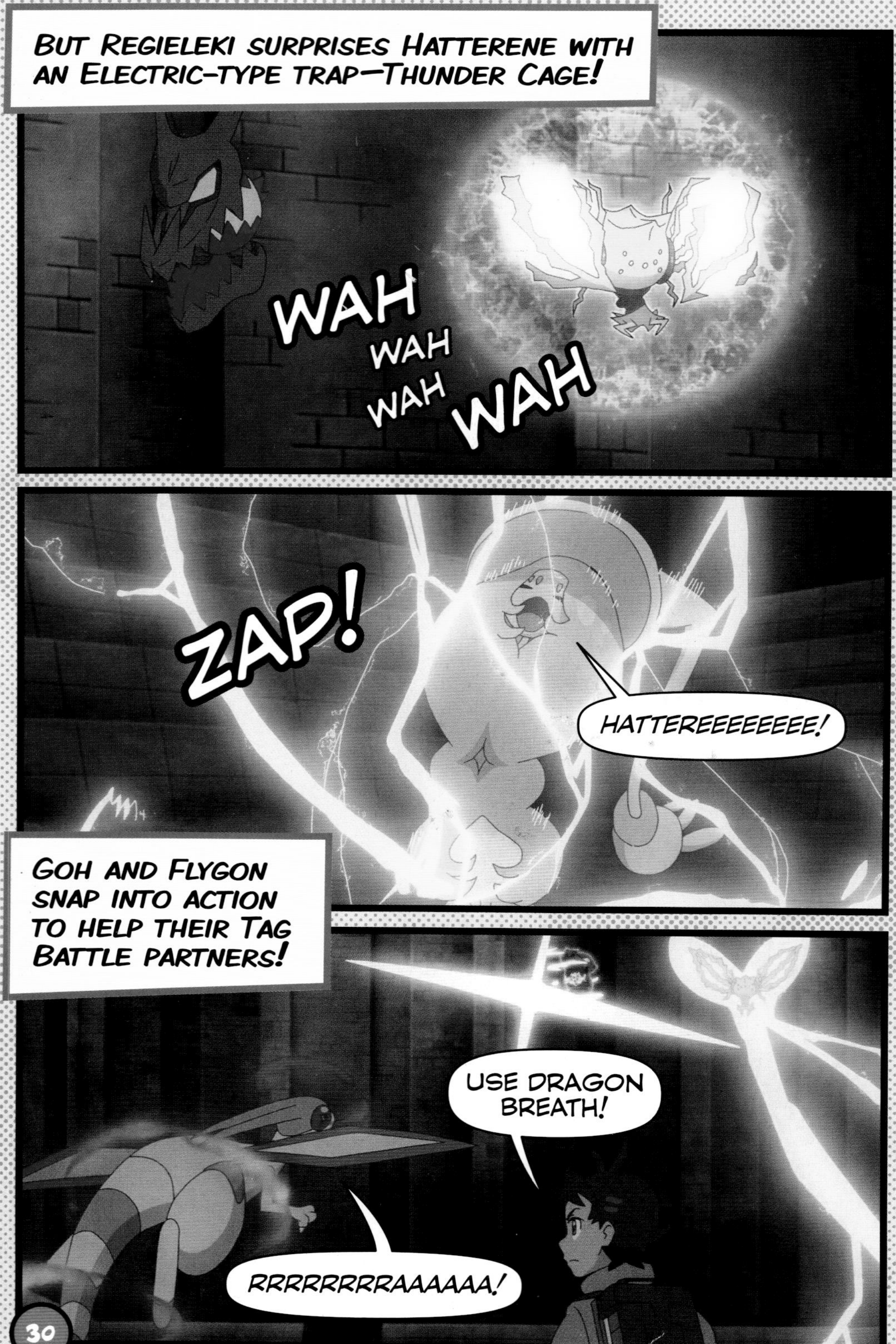

But Regieleki surprises Hatterene with an Electric-type trap—Thunder Cage!
WAH
WAH
WAH
WAH
ZAP!
HATTEREEEEEEEE!
Goh and Flygon snap into action to help their Tag Battle partners!
USE DRAGON BREATH!
RRRRRRRRAAAAAA!

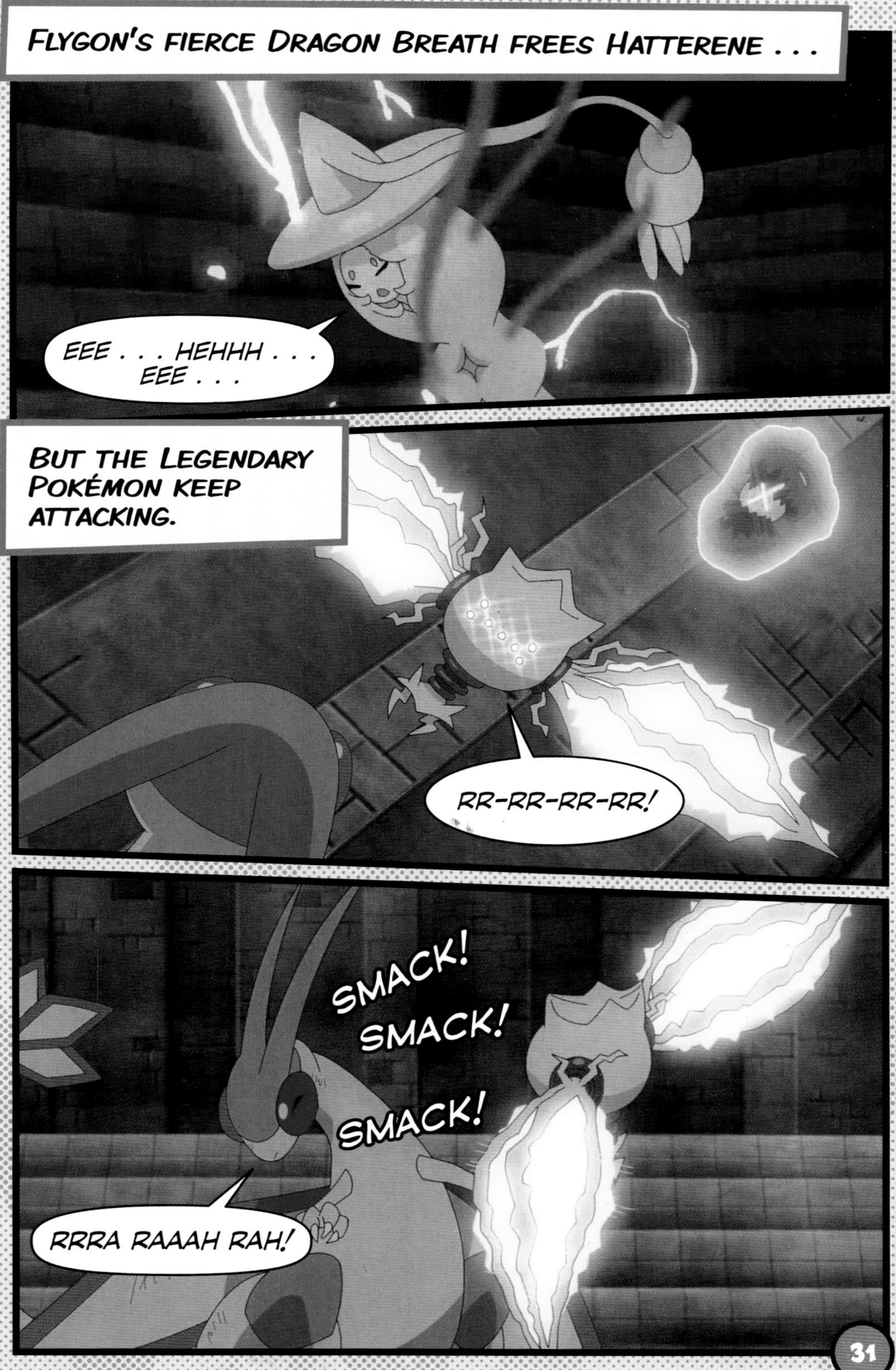
Flygon's fierce Dragon Breath frees Hatterene . . .
Eee . . . Hehhh . . . Eee . . .
But the Legendary Pokémon keep attacking.
RR-RR-RR-RR!
SMACK!
SMACK!
SMACK!
RRRA RAAAH RAH!

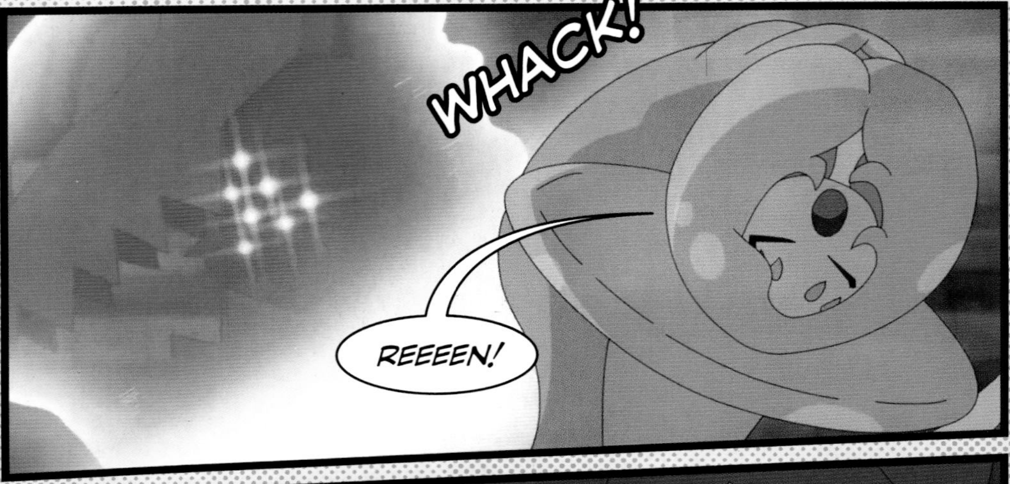
WHACK!
REEEEN!

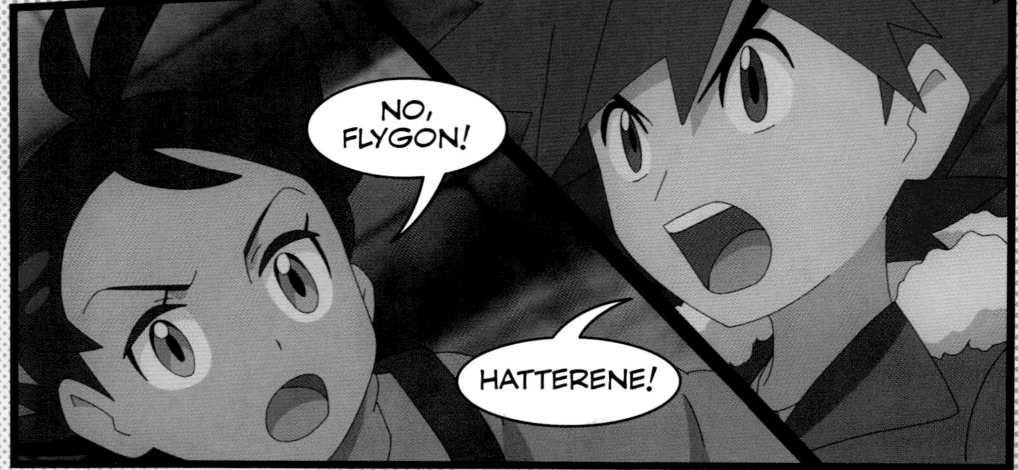
NO, FLYGON!
HATTERENE!

FLYGON AND HATTERENE GAVE THEIR ALL IN THE BATTLE WITH THE LEGENDARY POKÉMON, BUT THEY CAN'T CONTINUE. THEY EACH RETURN TO THEIR POKÉ BALLS.

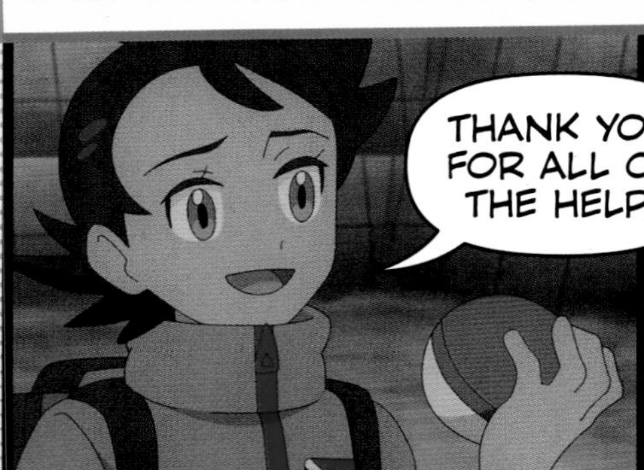
THANK YOU FOR ALL OF THE HELP.

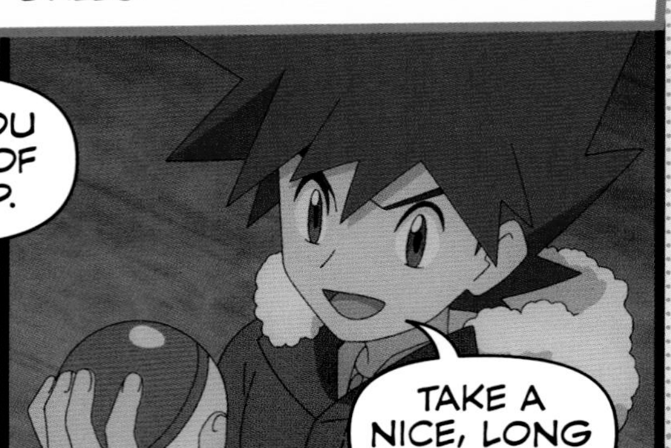
TAKE A NICE, LONG REST.

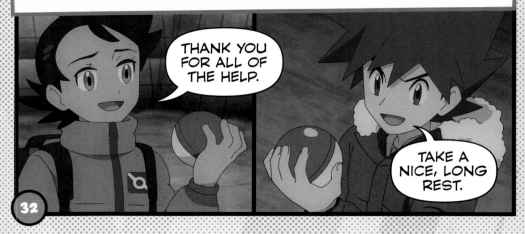

Gary and Goh have one more chance to win this epic battle with the Legendary Pokémon . . .

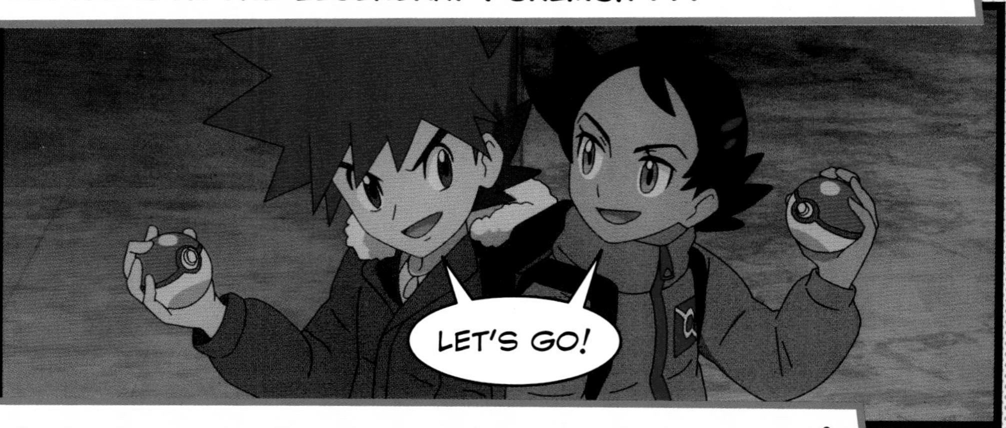
LET'S GO!

Cinderace and Blastoise are back with a roar!

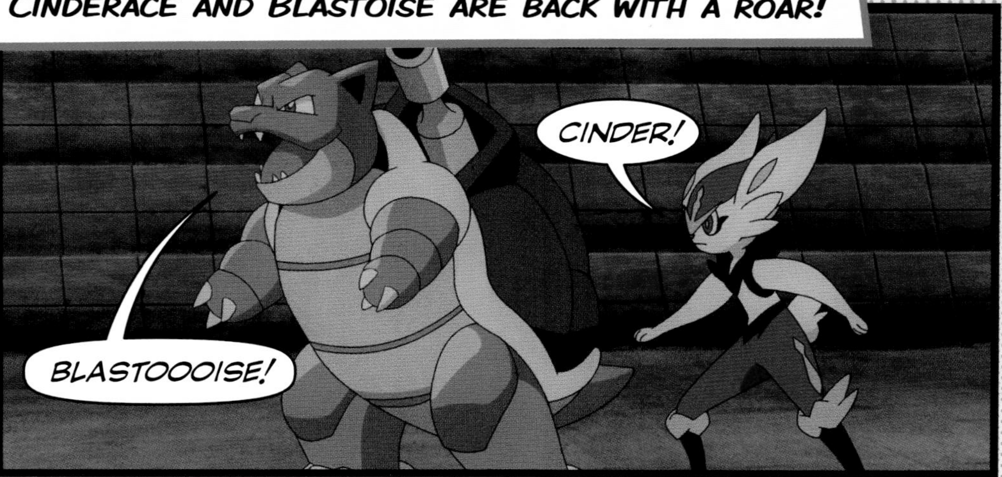
CINDER!
BLASTOOOOISE!

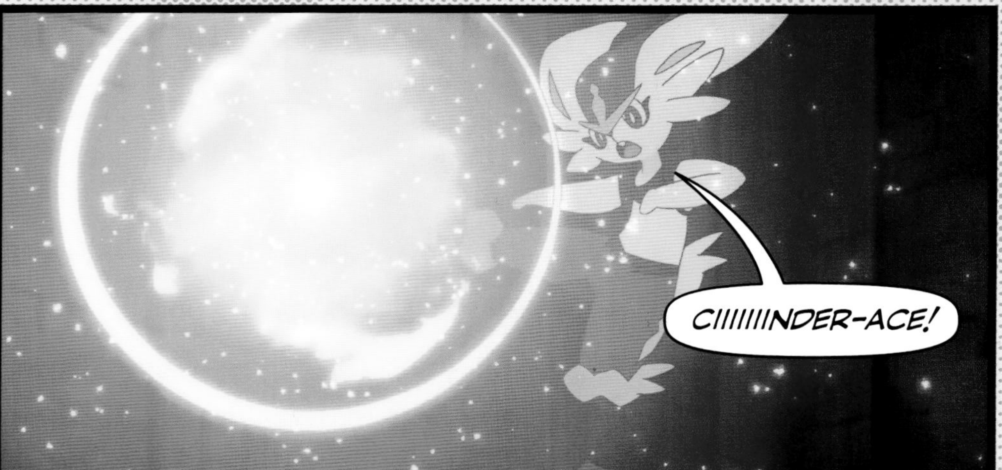
CIIIIIIINDER-ACE!

Cinderace prepares a powerful Pyro Ball . . .

WHOMP!

Blastoise tackles Regidrago in midair with Skull Bash!

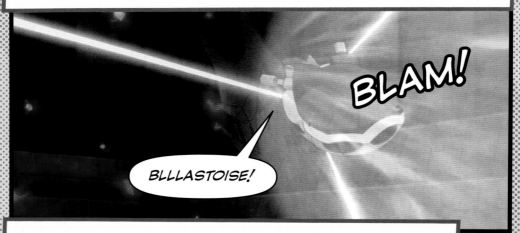

BLAM!

BLLLASTOISE!

Regieleki responds with a bright Zap Cannon . . .

ELELELE!

BUZZZZZAM!

34

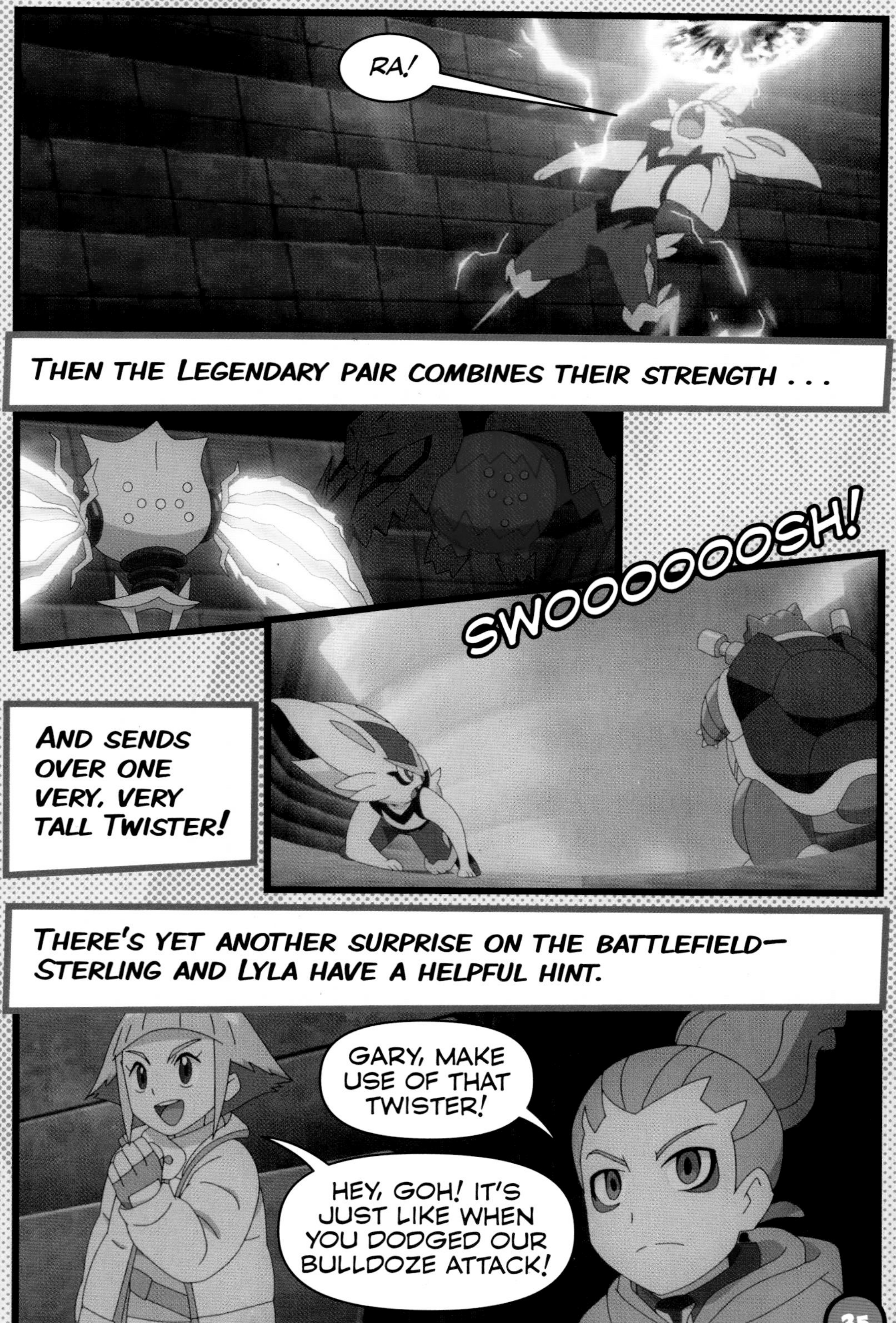
RA!
THEN THE LEGENDARY PAIR COMBINES THEIR STRENGTH . . .
SWOOOOOOOSH!
AND SENDS OVER ONE VERY, VERY TALL TWISTER!
THERE'S YET ANOTHER SURPRISE ON THE BATTLEFIELD— STERLING AND LYLA HAVE A HELPFUL HINT.
GARY, MAKE USE OF THAT TWISTER!
HEY, GOH! IT'S JUST LIKE WHEN YOU DODGED OUR BULLDOZE ATTACK!

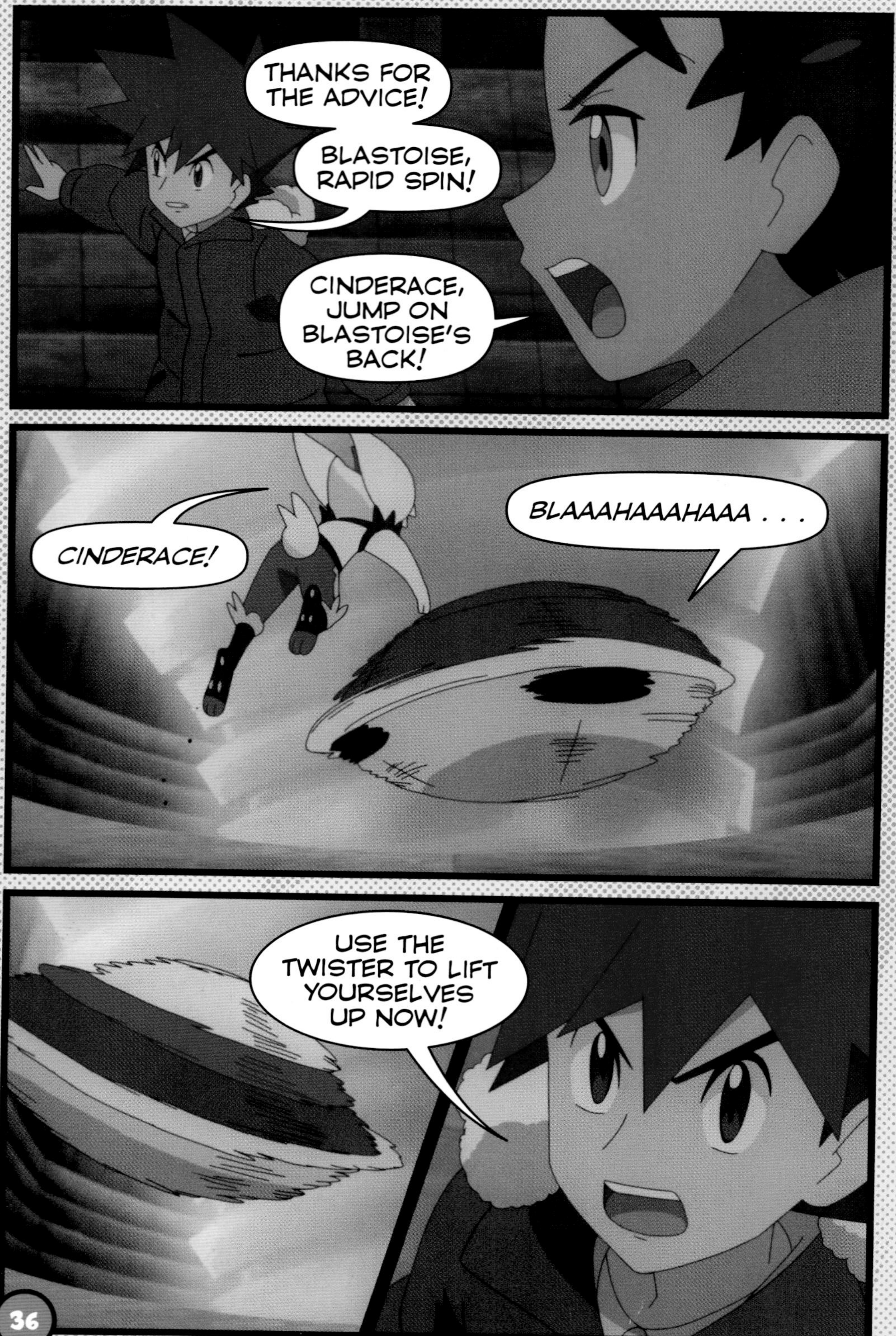
THANKS FOR THE ADVICE!
BLASTOISE, RAPID SPIN!
CINDERACE, JUMP ON BLASTOISE'S BACK!
CINDERACE!
BLAAAHAAAHAAA . . .
USE THE TWISTER TO LIFT YOURSELVES UP NOW!

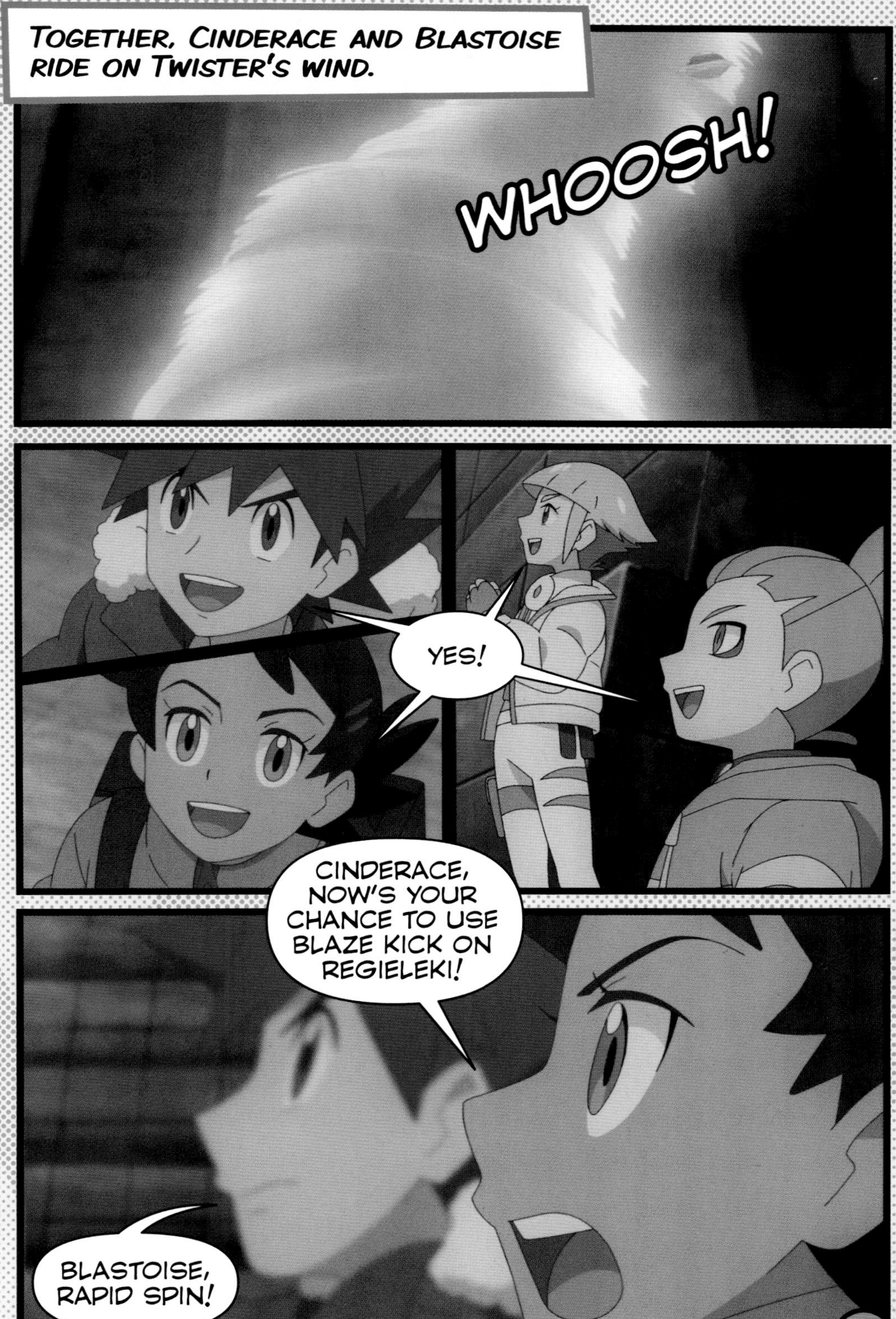
TOGETHER, CINDERACE AND BLASTOISE RIDE ON TWISTER'S WIND.
WHOOSH!
YES!
CINDERACE, NOW'S YOUR CHANCE TO USE BLAZE KICK ON REGIELEKI!
BLASTOISE, RAPID SPIN!

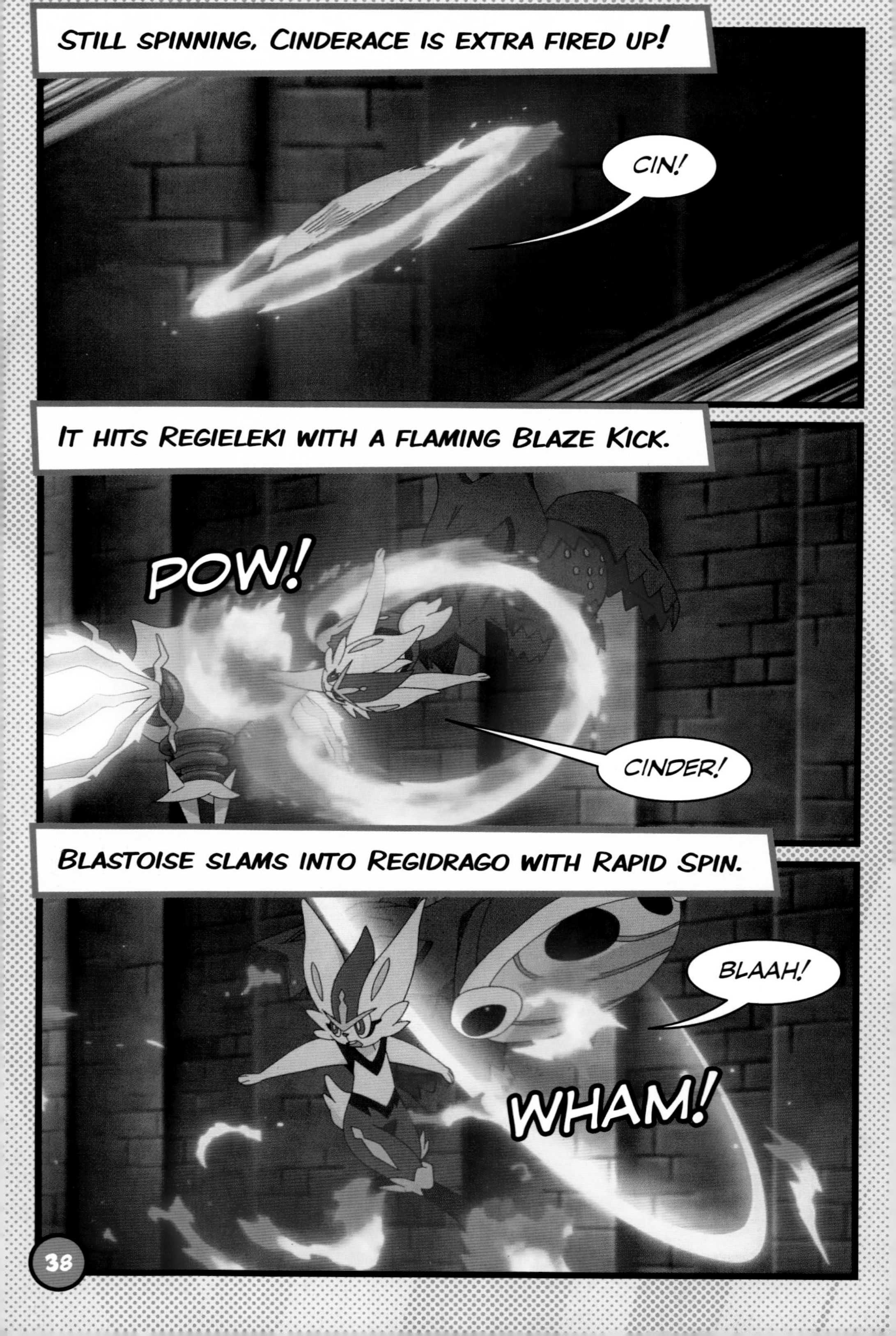
STILL SPINNING, CINDERACE IS EXTRA FIRED UP!
CIN!
IT HITS REGIELEKI WITH A FLAMING BLAZE KICK.
POW!
CINDER!
BLASTOISE SLAMS INTO REGIDRAGO WITH RAPID SPIN.
BLAAH!
WHAM!

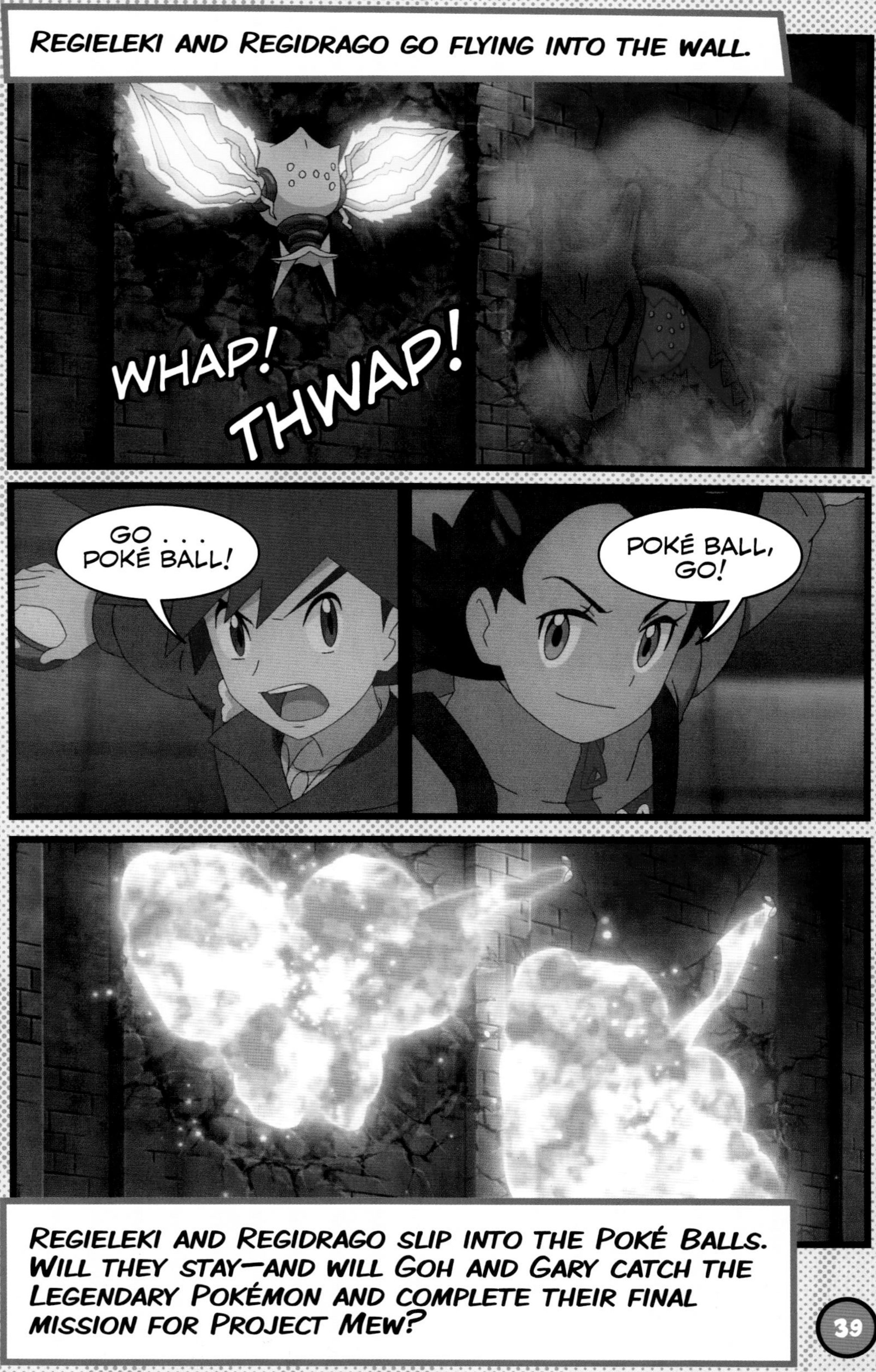
REGIELEKI AND REGIDRAGO GO FLYING INTO THE WALL.
WHAP!
THWAP!
GO . . . POKÉ BALL!
POKÉ BALL, GO!
REGIELEKI AND REGIDRAGO SLIP INTO THE POKÉ BALLS. WILL THEY STAY—AND WILL GOH AND GARY CATCH THE LEGENDARY POKÉMON AND COMPLETE THEIR FINAL MISSION FOR PROJECT MEW?

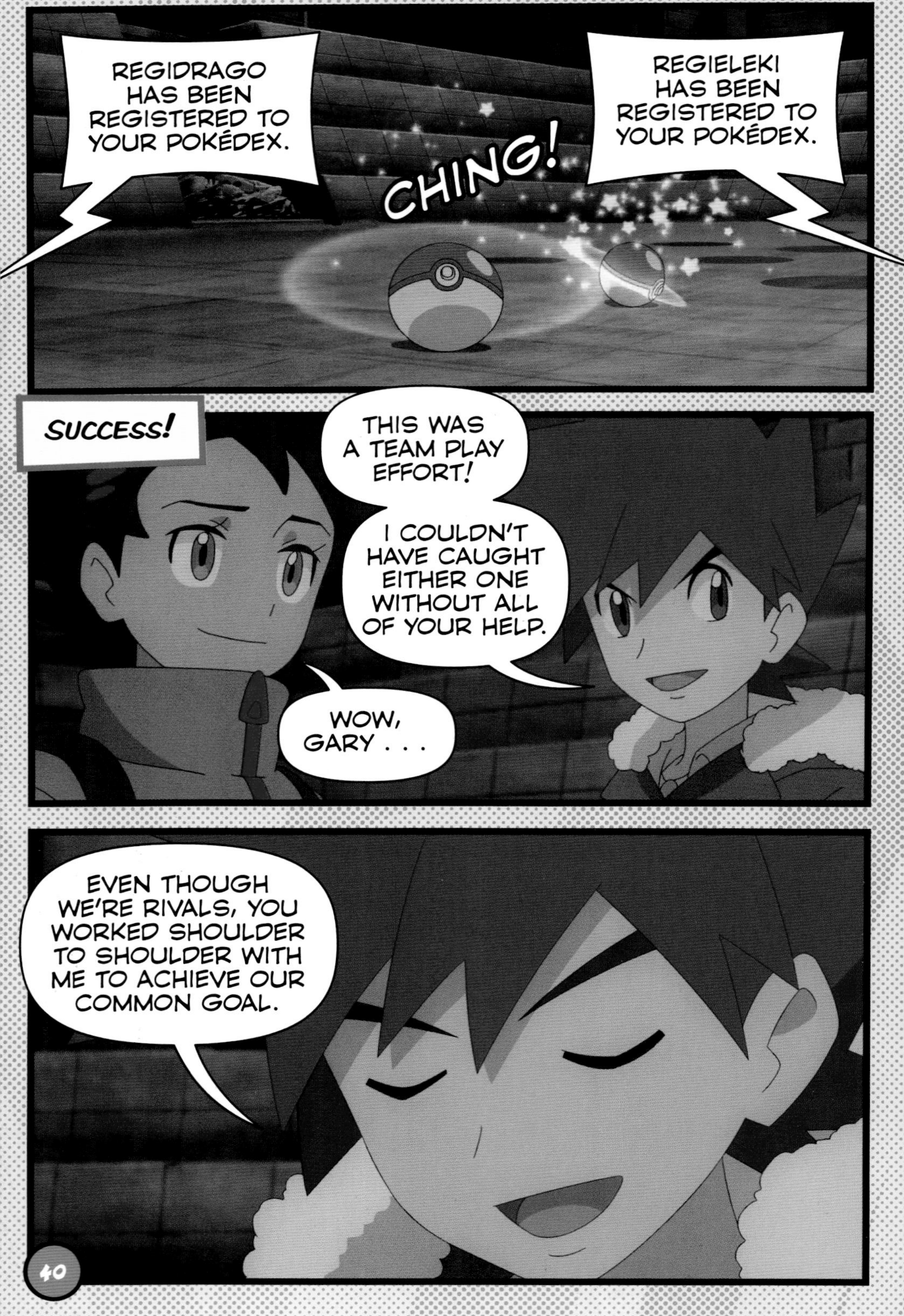
REGIDRAGO HAS BEEN REGISTERED TO YOUR POKÉDEX.
CHING!
REGIELEKI HAS BEEN REGISTERED TO YOUR POKÉDEX.
SUCCESS!
THIS WAS A TEAM PLAY EFFORT!
I COULDN'T HAVE CAUGHT EITHER ONE WITHOUT ALL OF YOUR HELP.
WOW, GARY . . .
EVEN THOUGH WE'RE RIVALS, YOU WORKED SHOULDER TO SHOULDER WITH ME TO ACHIEVE OUR COMMON GOAL.

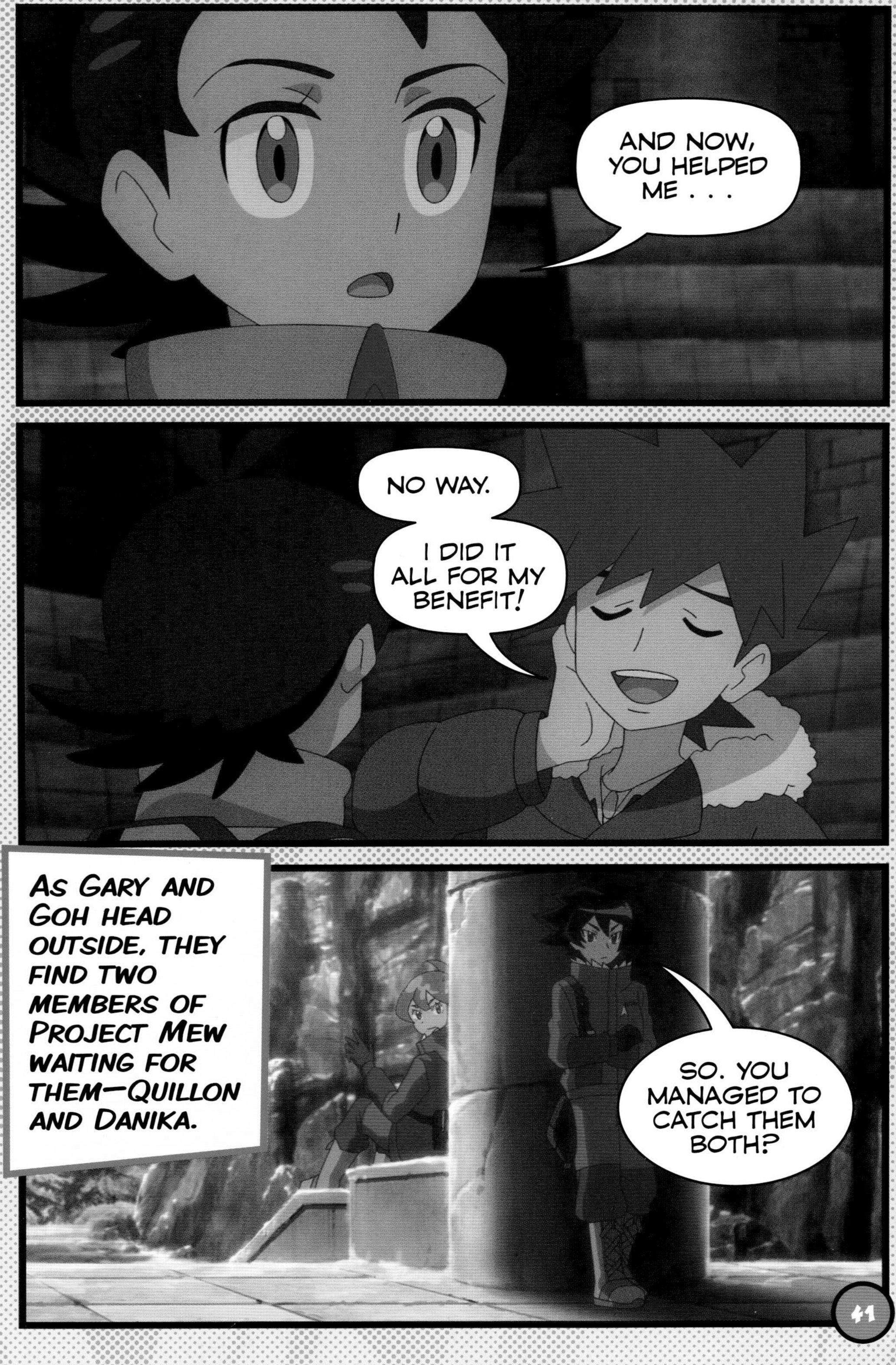
AND NOW, YOU HELPED ME . . .
NO WAY.
I DID IT ALL FOR MY BENEFIT!
AS GARY AND GOH HEAD OUTSIDE, THEY FIND TWO MEMBERS OF PROJECT MEW WAITING FOR THEM—QUILLON AND DANIKA.
SO. YOU MANAGED TO CATCH THEM BOTH?

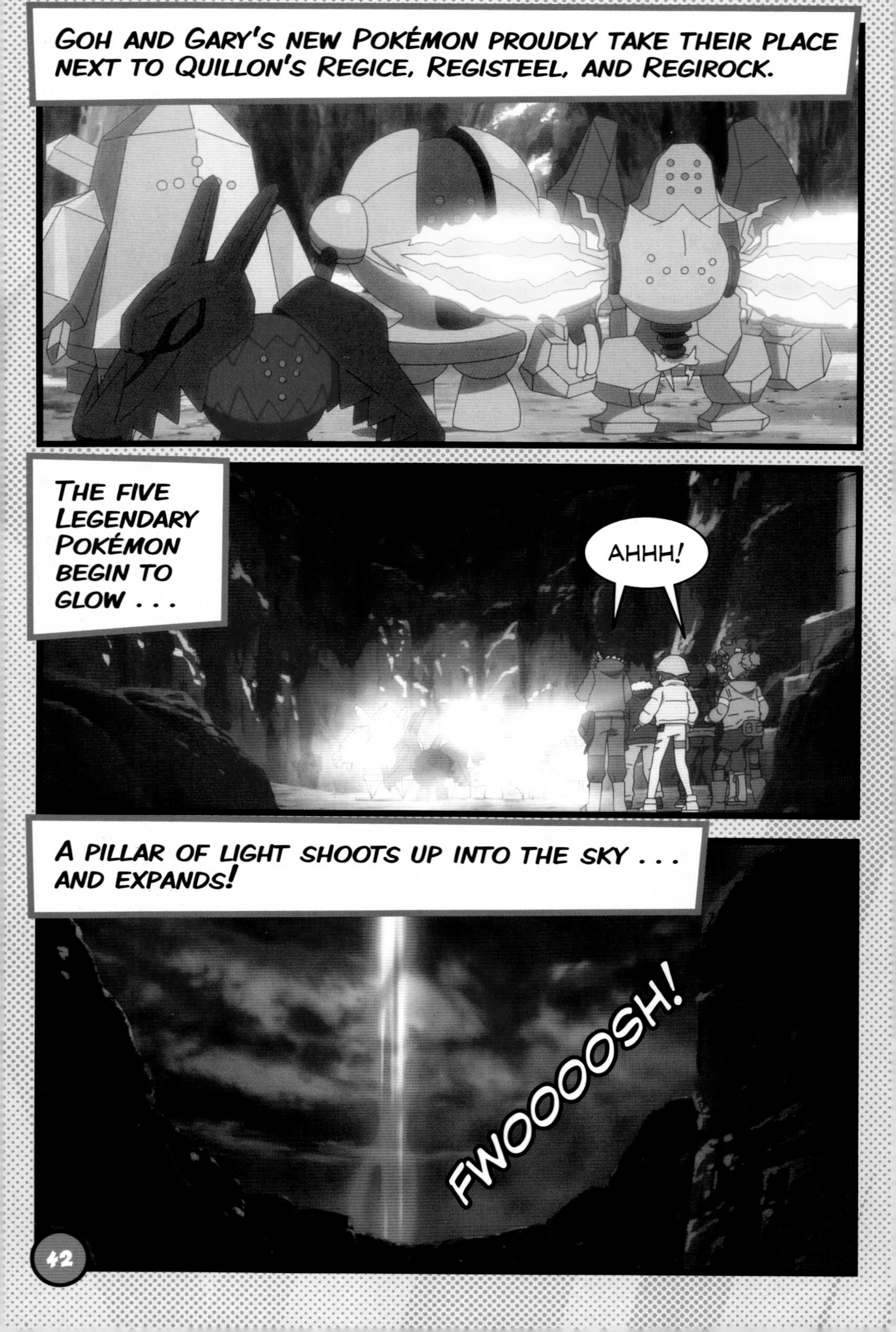
GOH AND GARY'S NEW POKÉMON PROUDLY TAKE THEIR PLACE NEXT TO QUILLON'S REGICE, REGISTEEL, AND REGIROCK.
THE FIVE LEGENDARY POKÉMON BEGIN TO GLOW . . .
AHHH!
A PILLAR OF LIGHT SHOOTS UP INTO THE SKY . . . AND EXPANDS!
FWOOOOSH!

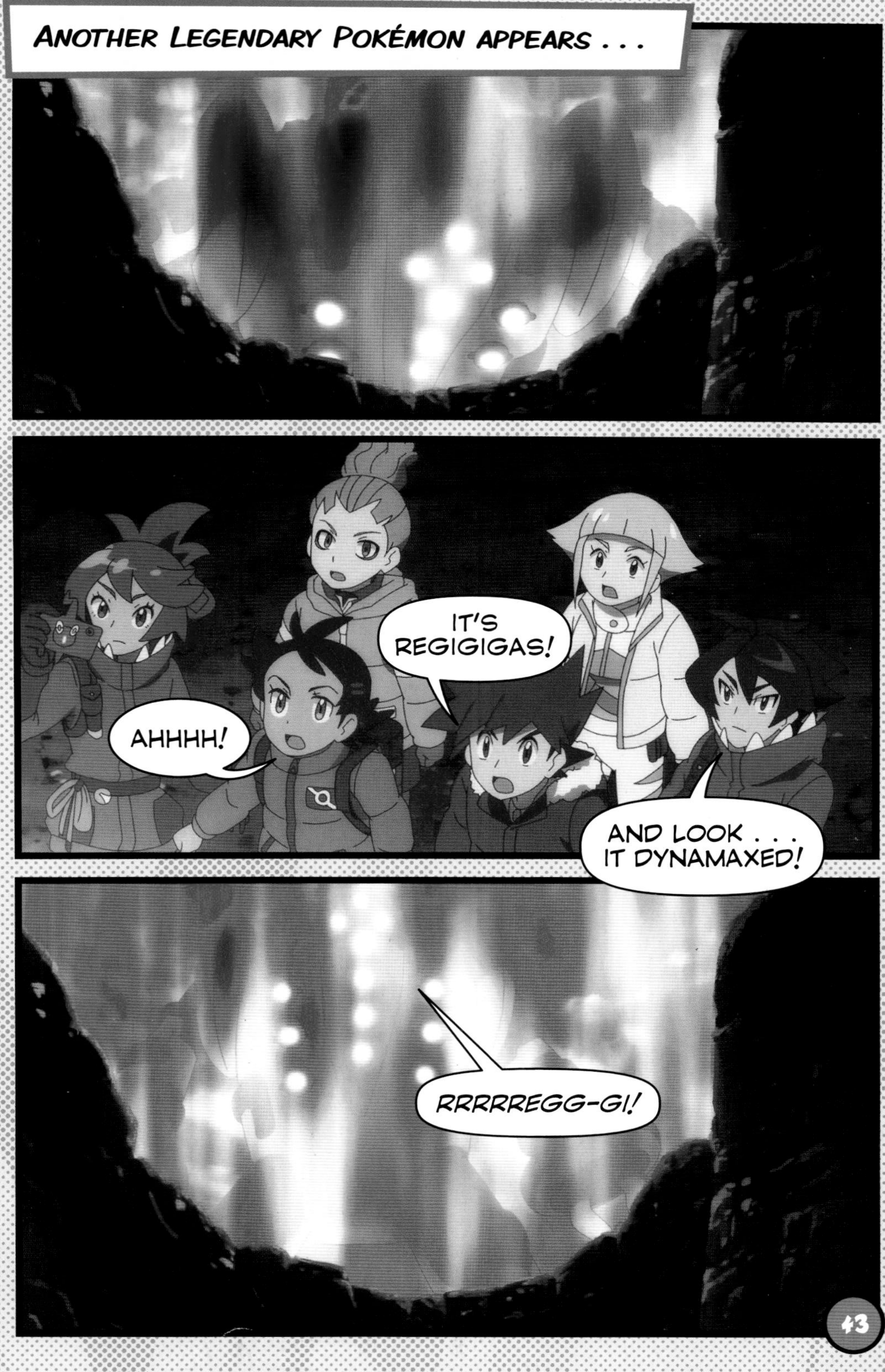
ANOTHER LEGENDARY POKÉMON APPEARS . . .
AHHHH!
IT'S REGIGIGAS!
AND LOOK . . . IT DYNAMAXED!
RRRRREGG-GI!

Then, as quickly as it appeared, Regigigas disappears.

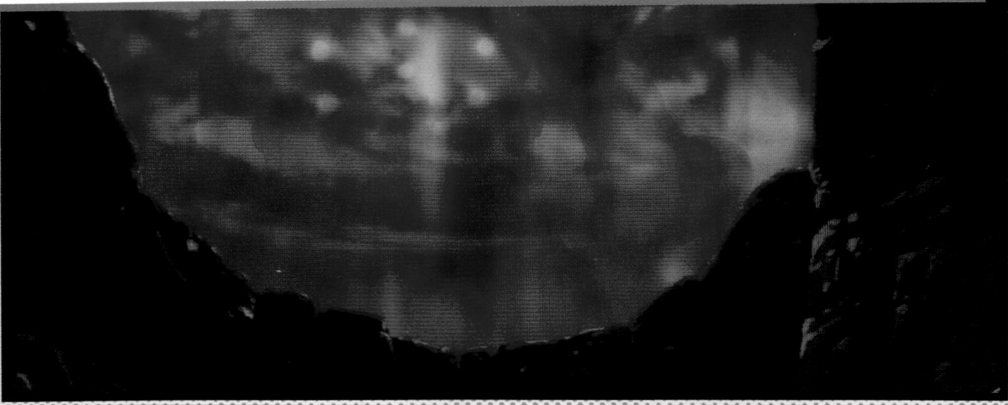

The day is back to normal—well, as normal as a day with six Legendary Pokémon, a Dynamax, two epic battles, and a Project Mew mission could be . . .

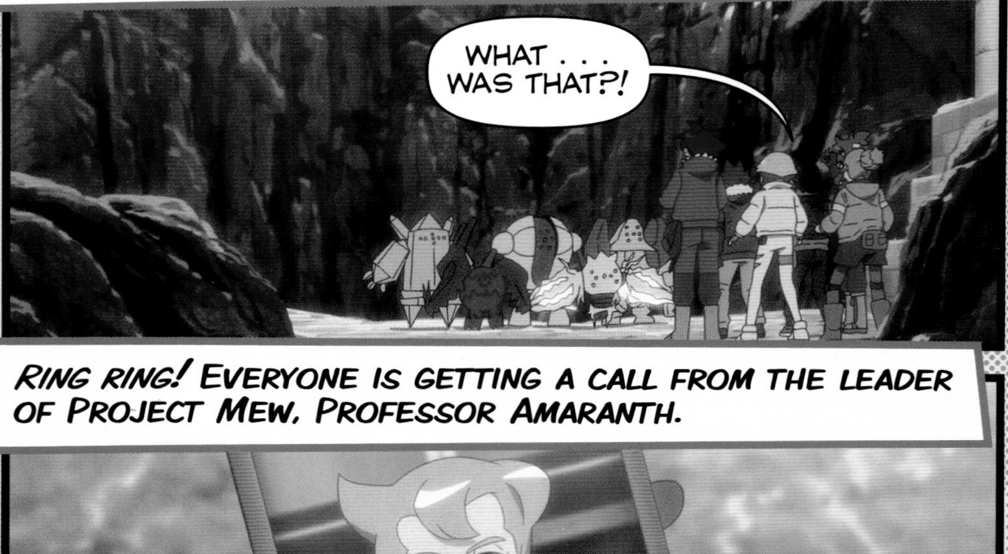

WHAT . . . WAS THAT?!

Ring ring! Everyone is getting a call from the leader of Project Mew, Professor Amaranth.

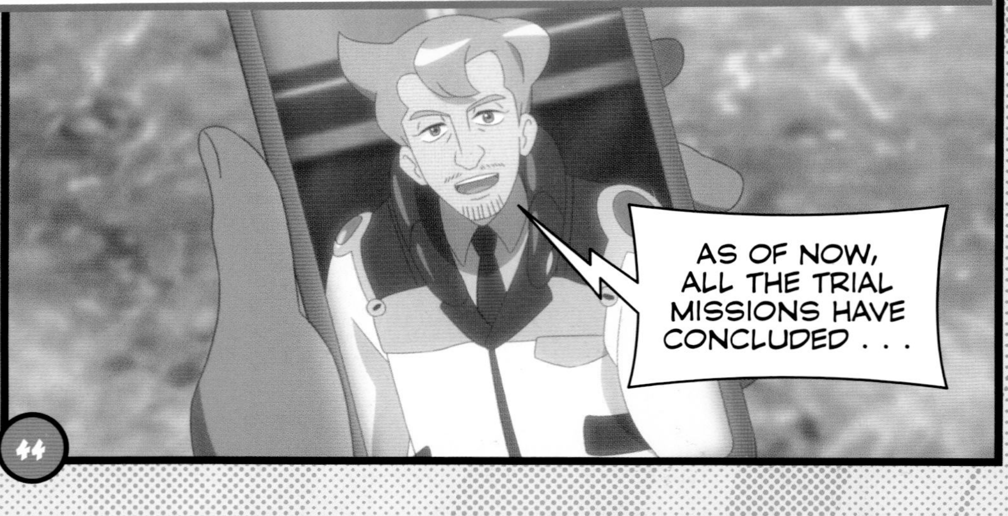

AS OF NOW, ALL THE TRIAL MISSIONS HAVE CONCLUDED . . .

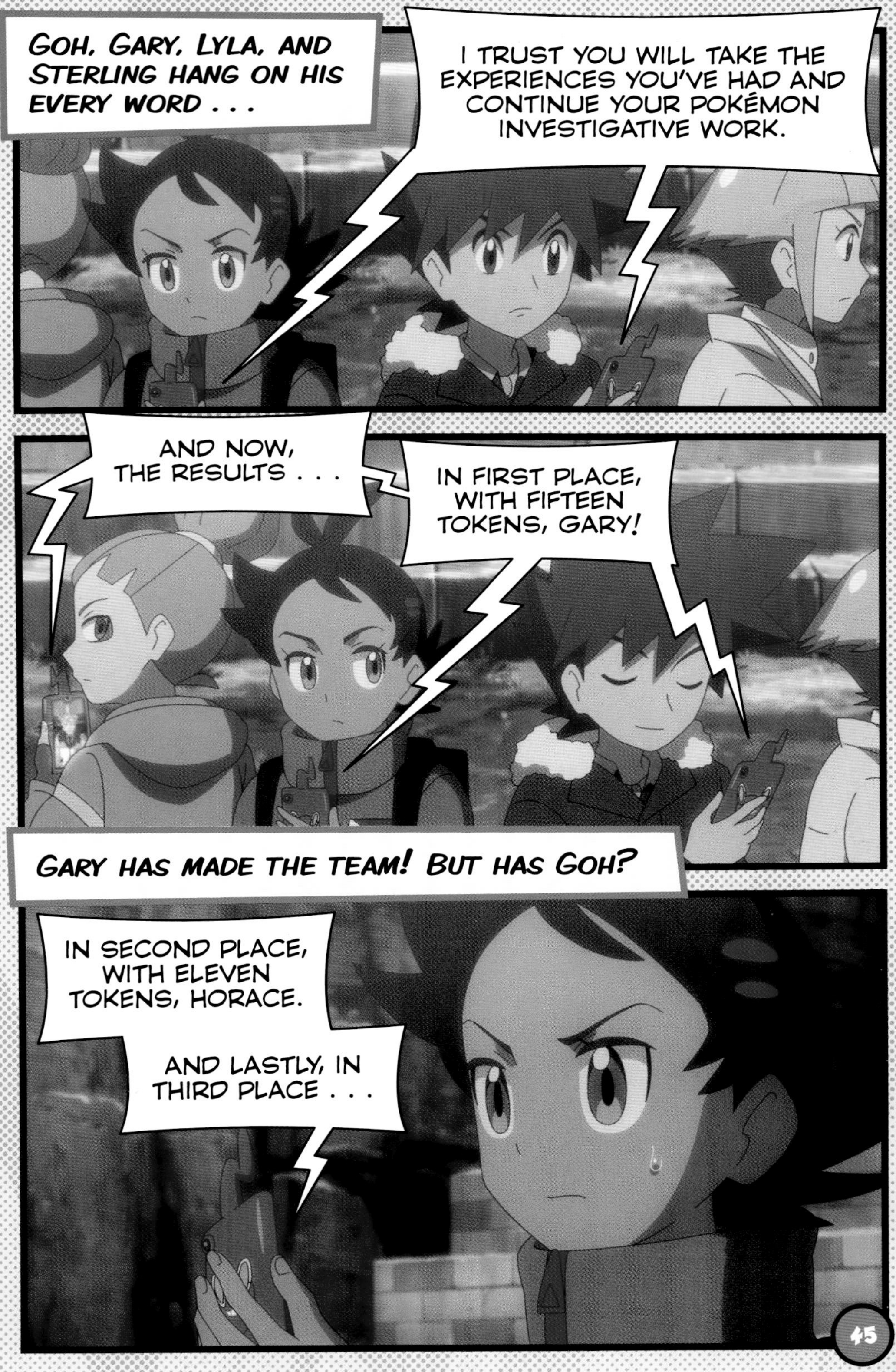
GOH, GARY, LYLA, AND STERLING HANG ON HIS EVERY WORD . . .
I TRUST YOU WILL TAKE THE EXPERIENCES YOU'VE HAD AND CONTINUE YOUR POKÉMON INVESTIGATIVE WORK.
AND NOW, THE RESULTS . . .
IN FIRST PLACE, WITH FIFTEEN TOKENS, GARY!
GARY HAS MADE THE TEAM! BUT HAS GOH?
IN SECOND PLACE, WITH ELEVEN TOKENS, HORACE.
AND LASTLY, IN THIRD PLACE . . .

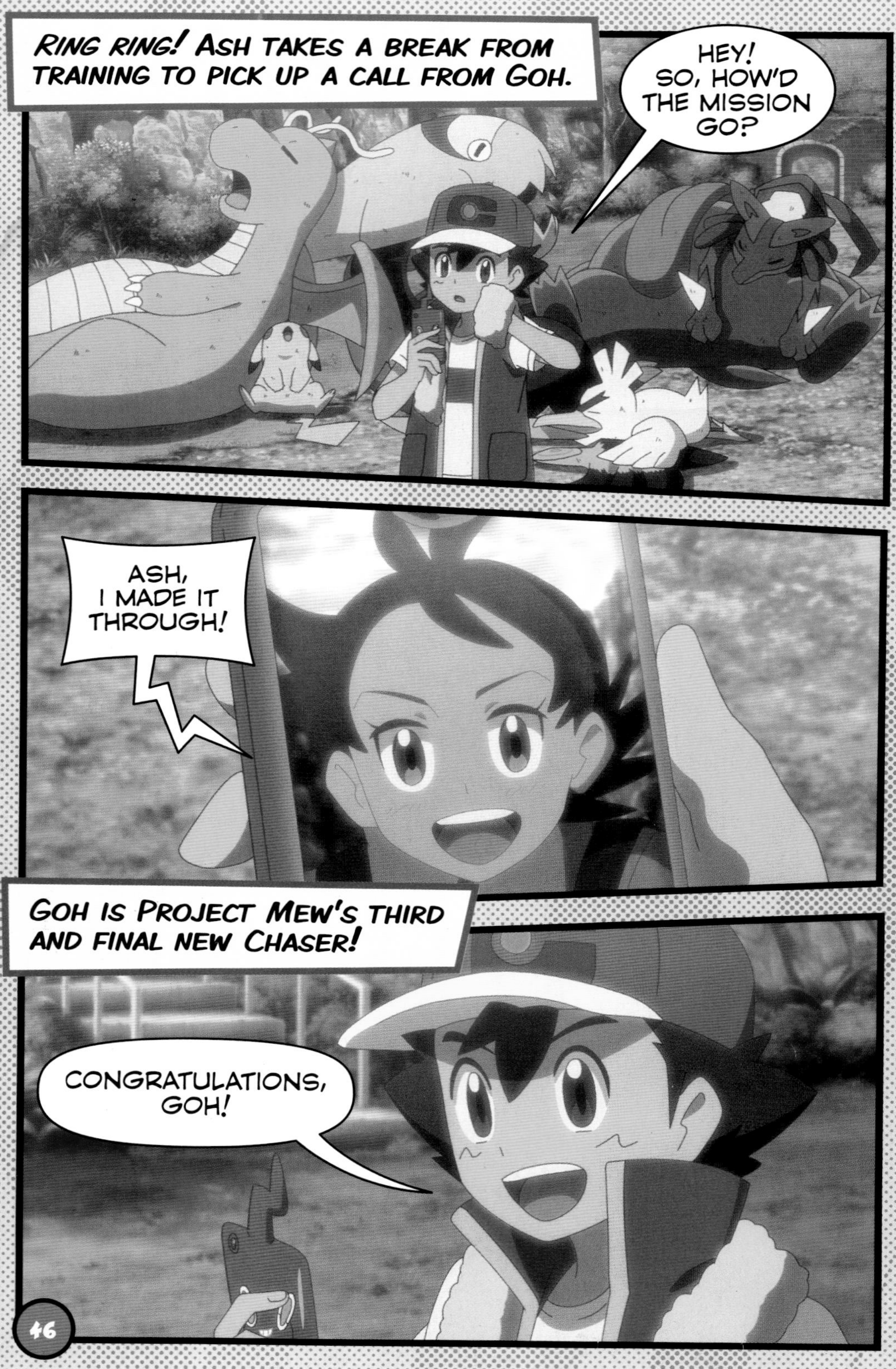
RING RING! ASH TAKES A BREAK FROM TRAINING TO PICK UP A CALL FROM GOH.
HEY! SO, HOW'D THE MISSION GO?
ASH, I MADE IT THROUGH!
GOH IS PROJECT MEW'S THIRD AND FINAL NEW CHASER!
CONGRATULATIONS, GOH!

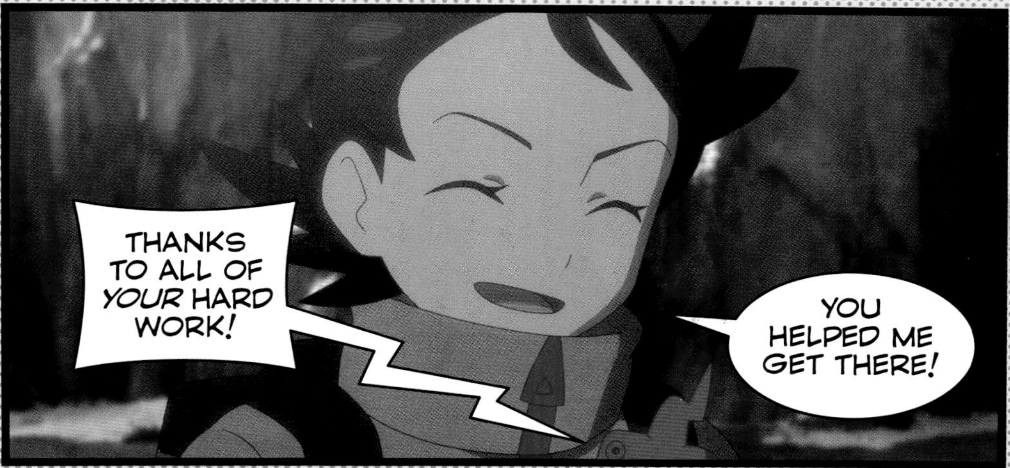
THANKS TO ALL OF *YOUR* HARD WORK!
YOU HELPED ME GET THERE!

GOH FEELS READY TO TAKE ON ANY CHALLENGE WITH HIS NEW TEAMMATES AND OLD FRIENDS AT PROJECT MEW.

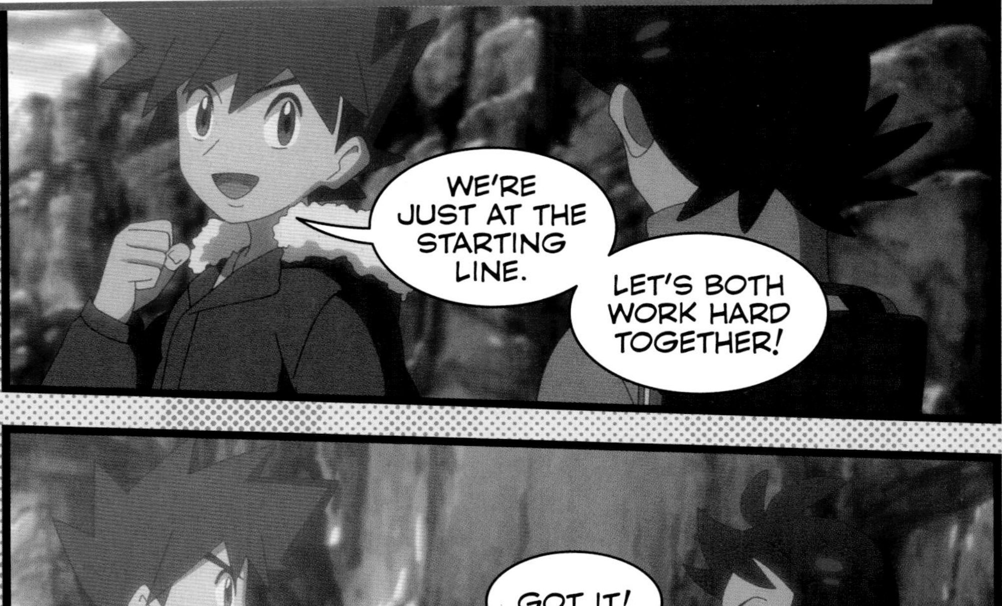
WE'RE JUST AT THE STARTING LINE.
LET'S BOTH WORK HARD TOGETHER!

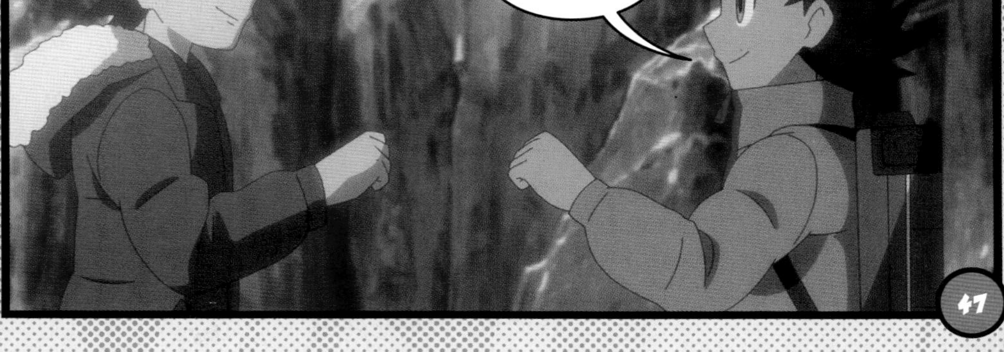
GOT IT!

Training to Win

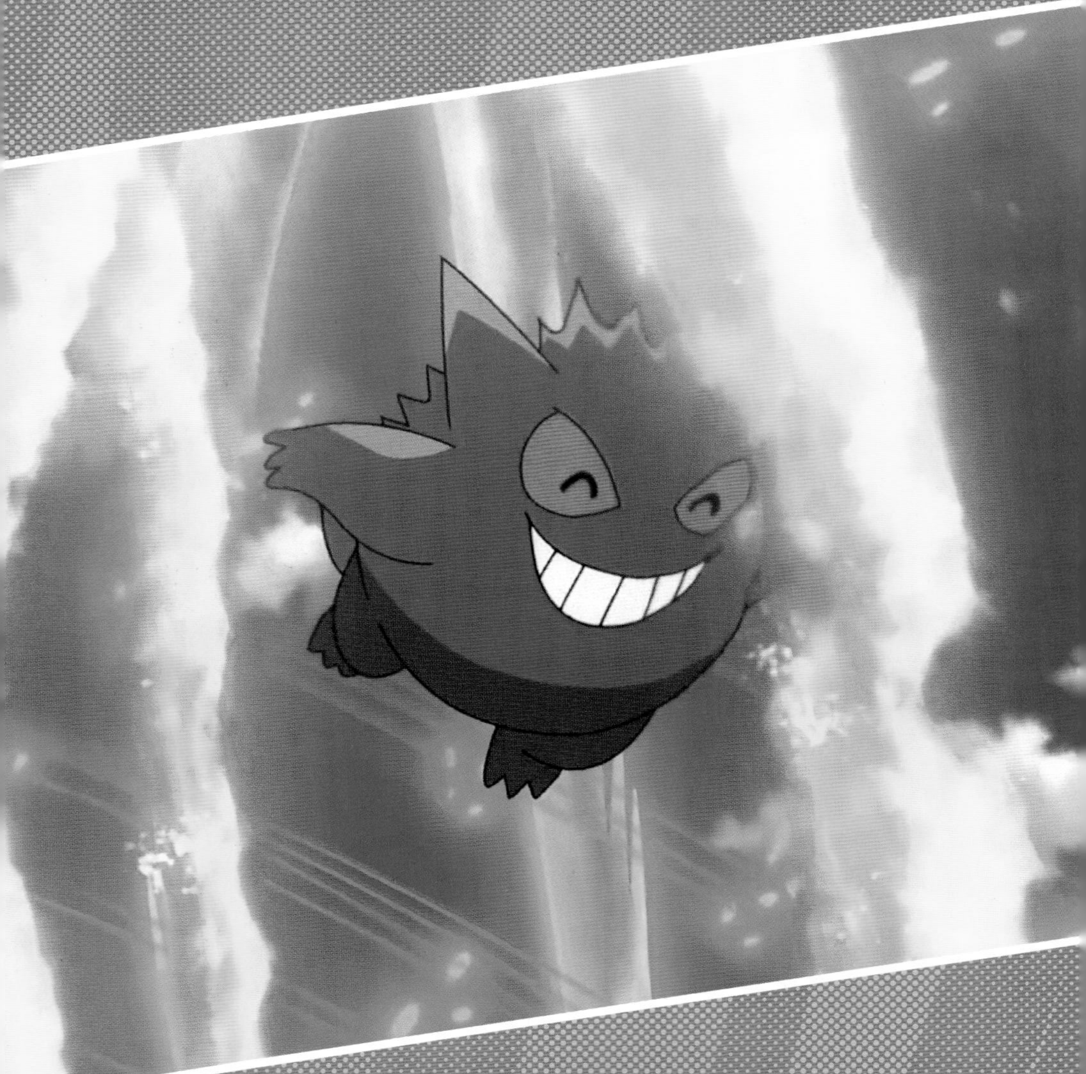

ASH AND HIS POKÉMON ARE TRAINING HARD TO PREPARE FOR BATTLE IN THE EPIC MASTERS EIGHT TOURNAMENT OF THE WORLD CORONATION SERIES.

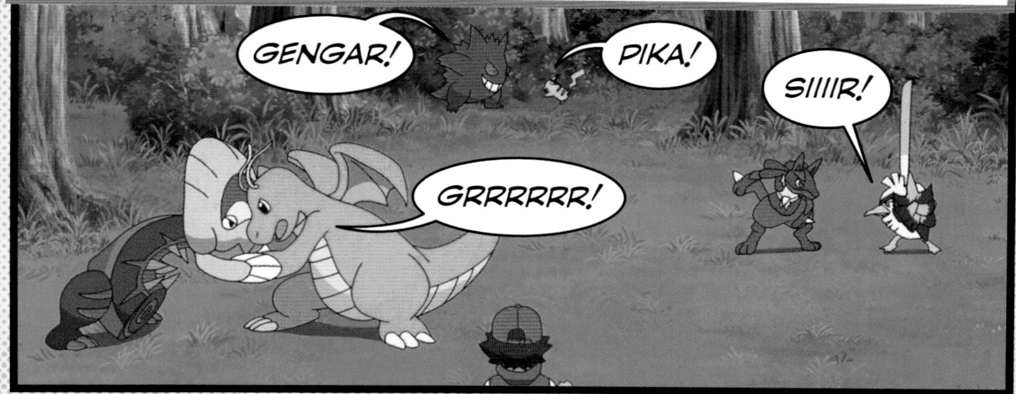
GENGAR!
PIKA!
SIIIIR!
GRRRRRR!

ASH KNOWS THERE IS NOTHING LIKE SEEING OLD FRIENDS TO LIFT YOUR SPIRITS. SO HE'S PLANNING A BIG SURPRISE POKÉMON REUNION AT PROFESSOR OAK'S LAB BEFORE THE TOURNAMENT!

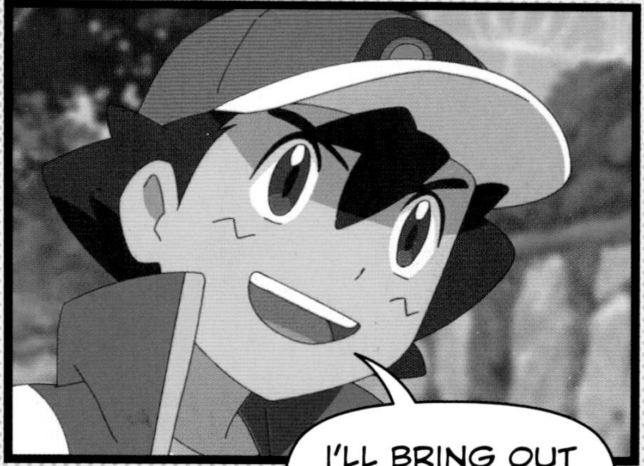
I'LL BRING OUT THEIR BATTLING SPIRIT AND MINE, TOO!

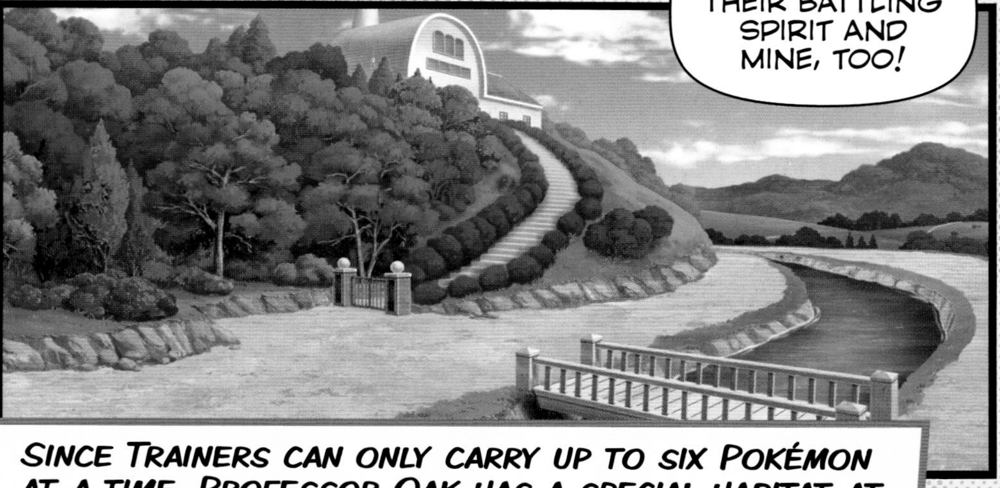

SINCE TRAINERS CAN ONLY CARRY UP TO SIX POKÉMON AT A TIME, PROFESSOR OAK HAS A SPECIAL HABITAT AT HIS LAB FOR THEIR OTHER POKÉMON TO LIVE IN.

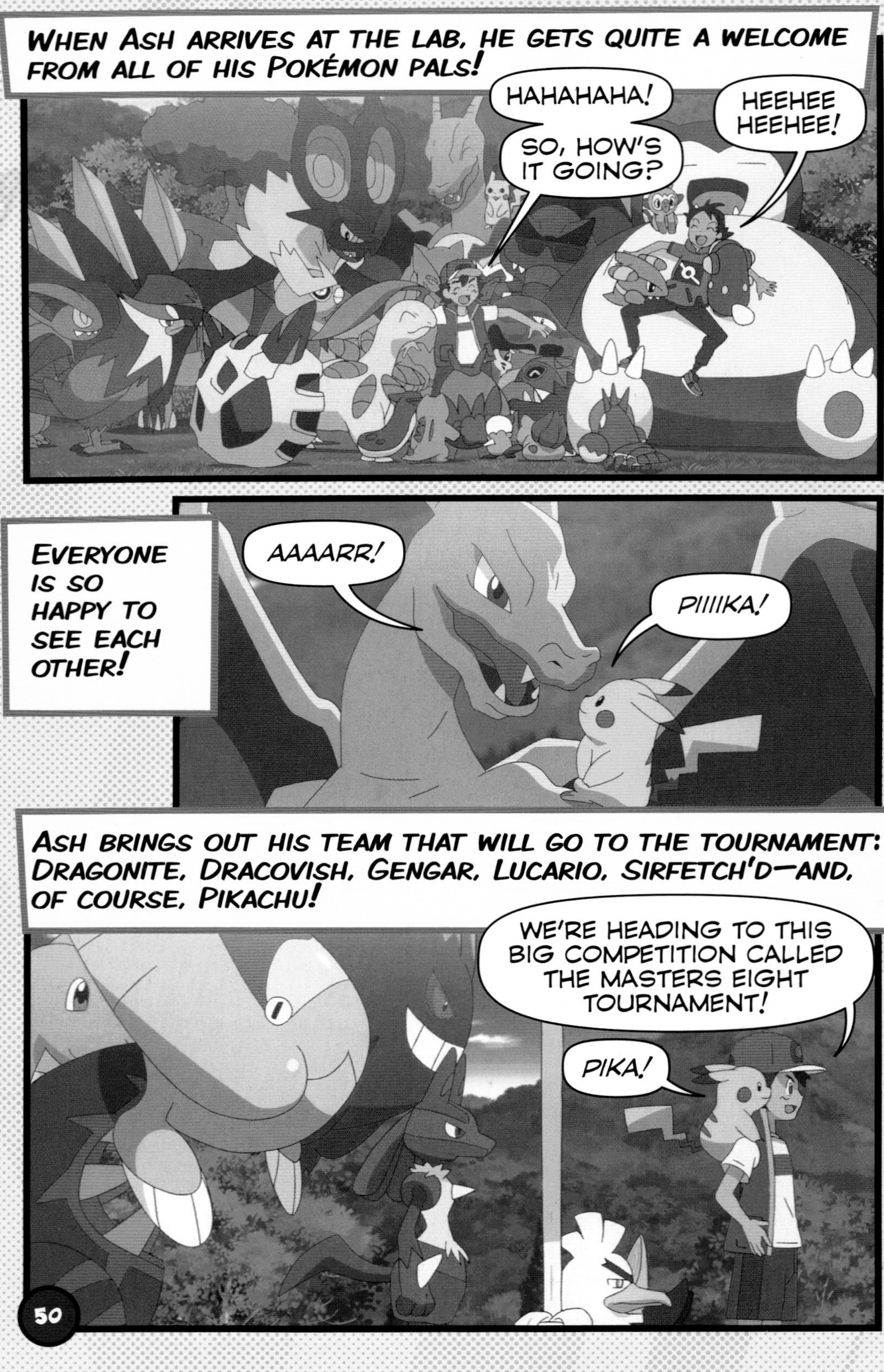
WHEN ASH ARRIVES AT THE LAB, HE GETS QUITE A WELCOME FROM ALL OF HIS POKÉMON PALS!
HAHAHAHA!
SO, HOW'S IT GOING?
HEEHEE HEEHEE!
EVERYONE IS SO HAPPY TO SEE EACH OTHER!
AAAARR!
PIIIIKA!
ASH BRINGS OUT HIS TEAM THAT WILL GO TO THE TOURNAMENT: DRAGONITE, DRACOVISH, GENGAR, LUCARIO, SIRFETCH'D—AND, OF COURSE, PIKACHU!
WE'RE HEADING TO THIS BIG COMPETITION CALLED THE MASTERS EIGHT TOURNAMENT!
PIKA!

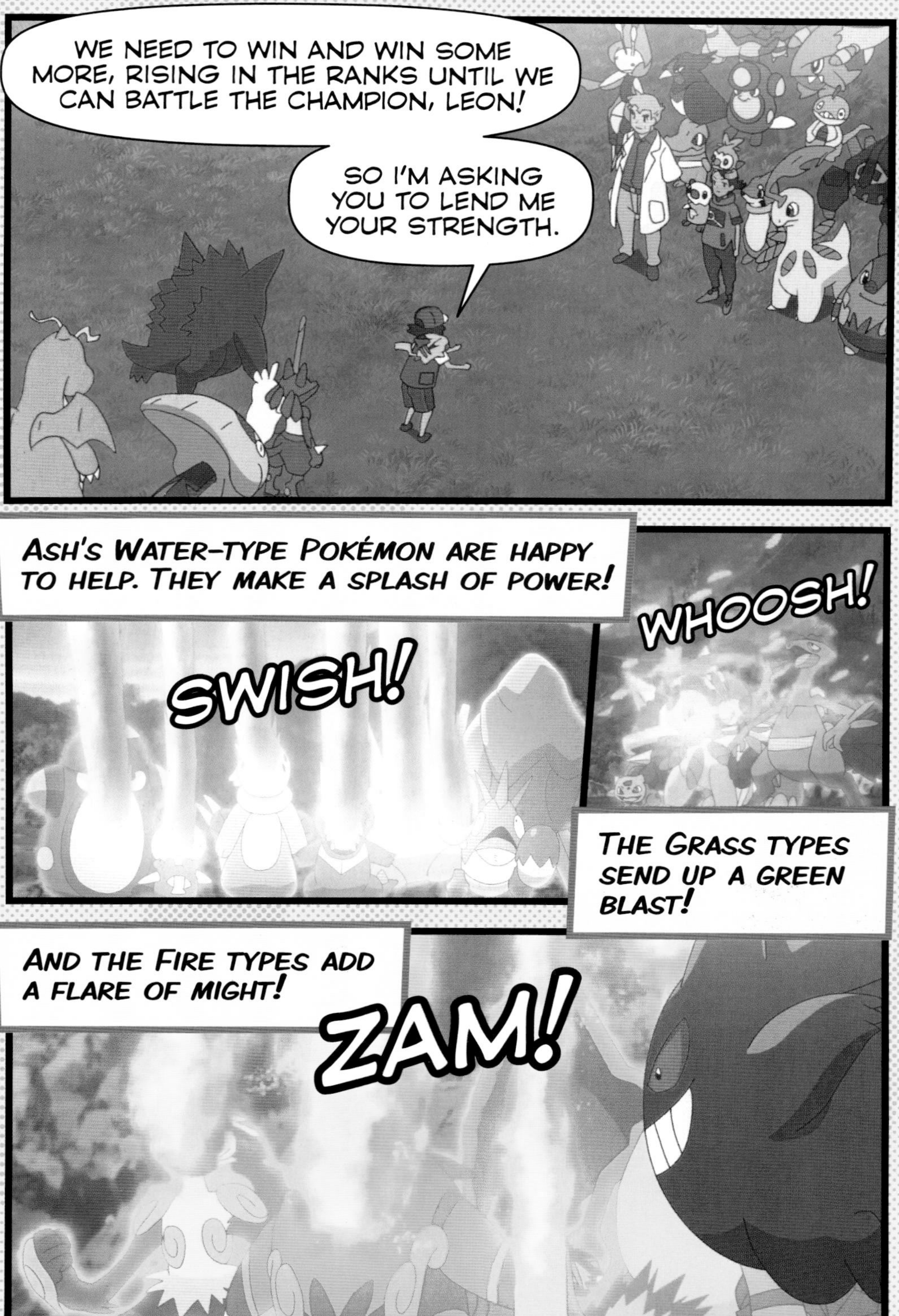
WE NEED TO WIN AND WIN SOME MORE, RISING IN THE RANKS UNTIL WE CAN BATTLE THE CHAMPION, LEON!
SO I'M ASKING YOU TO LEND ME YOUR STRENGTH.
ASH'S WATER-TYPE POKÉMON ARE HAPPY TO HELP. THEY MAKE A SPLASH OF POWER!
SWISH!
WHOOSH!
THE GRASS TYPES SEND UP A GREEN BLAST!
AND THE FIRE TYPES ADD A FLARE OF MIGHT!
ZAM!

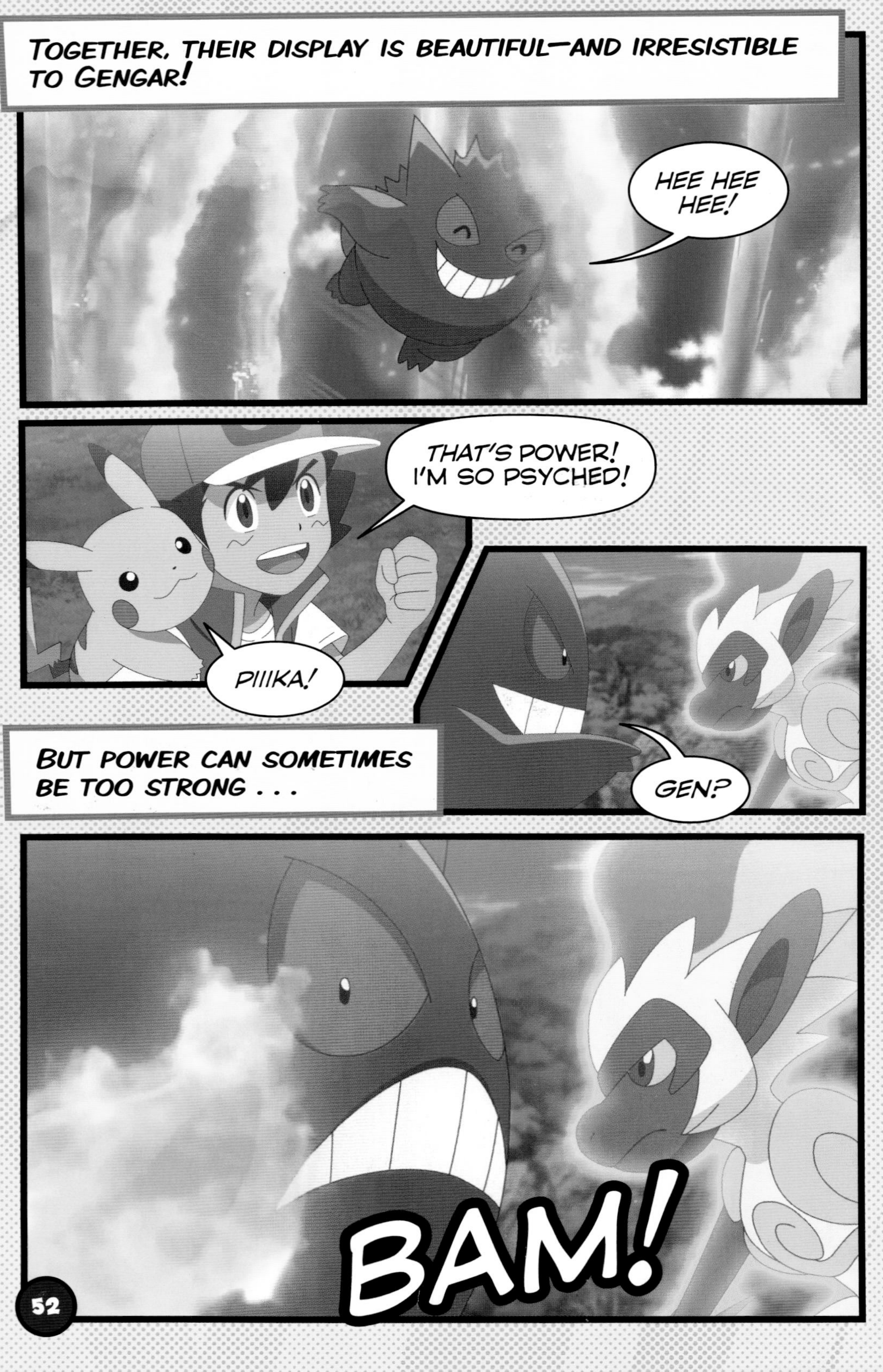
TOGETHER, THEIR DISPLAY IS BEAUTIFUL—AND IRRESISTIBLE TO GENGAR!
HEE HEE HEE!
THAT'S POWER! I'M SO PSYCHED!
PIIIKA!
GEN?
BUT POWER CAN SOMETIMES BE TOO STRONG . . .
BAM!

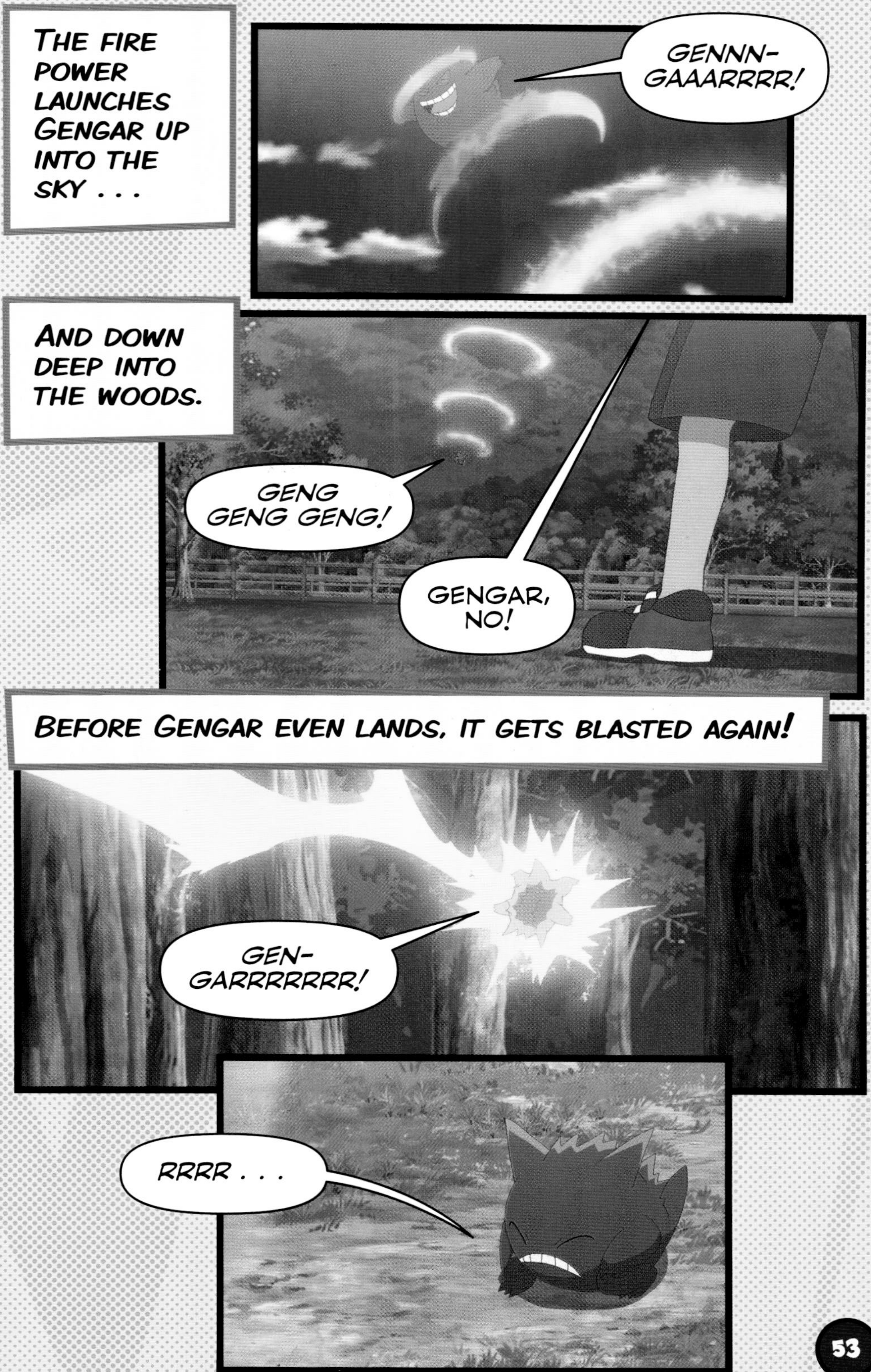
THE FIRE POWER LAUNCHES GENGAR UP INTO THE SKY . . .
GENNN-GAAARRRR!
AND DOWN DEEP INTO THE WOODS.
GENG GENG GENG!
GENGAR, NO!
BEFORE GENGAR EVEN LANDS, IT GETS BLASTED AGAIN!
GEN-GARRRRRRR!
RRRR . . .

Soon, Gengar is face-to-face with the Pokémon who zapped it—Electivire.

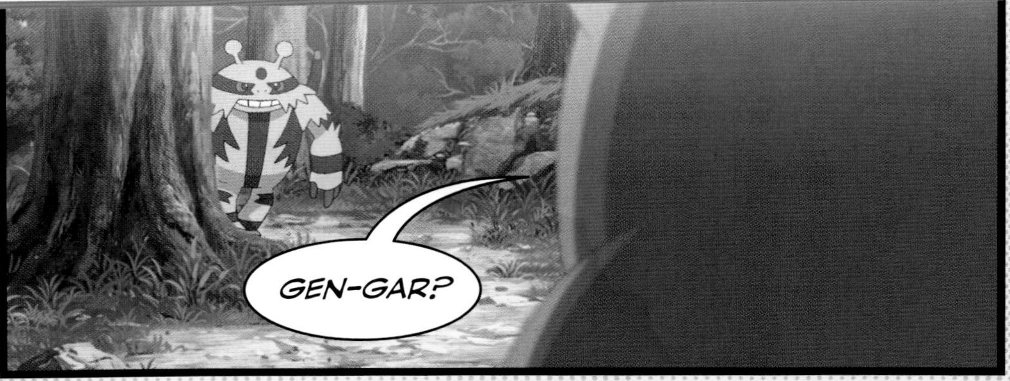
Gen-gar?

When Ash, Goh, Pikachu, and Grookey finally catch up, they see Gengar is not alone . . .

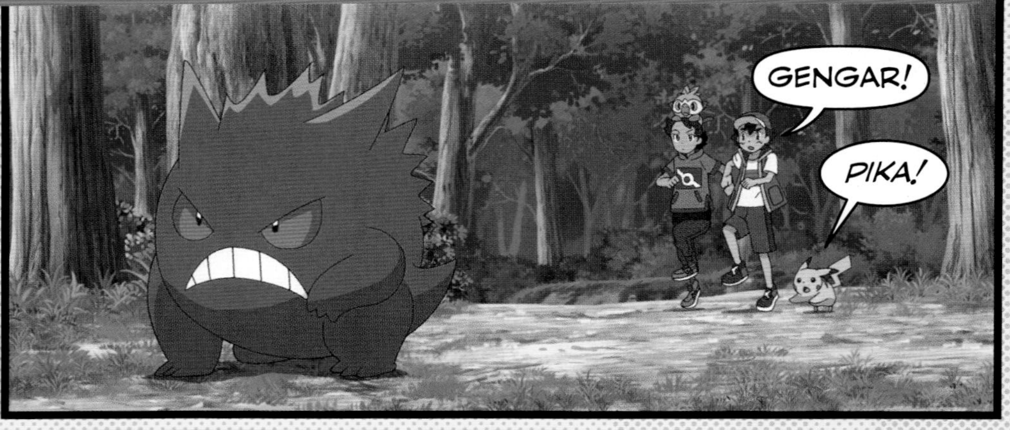
Gengar!
Pika!

It's Ash's old rival from the Sinnoh region, Paul.

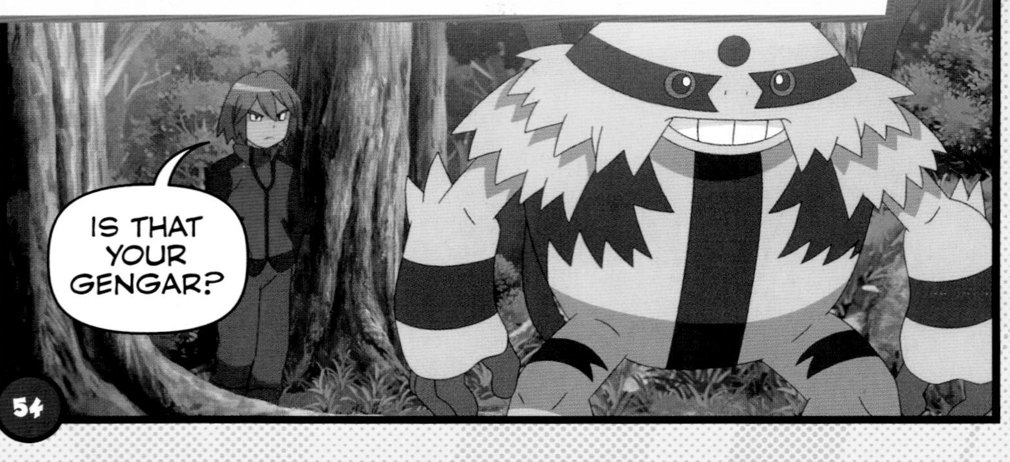
Is that your Gengar?

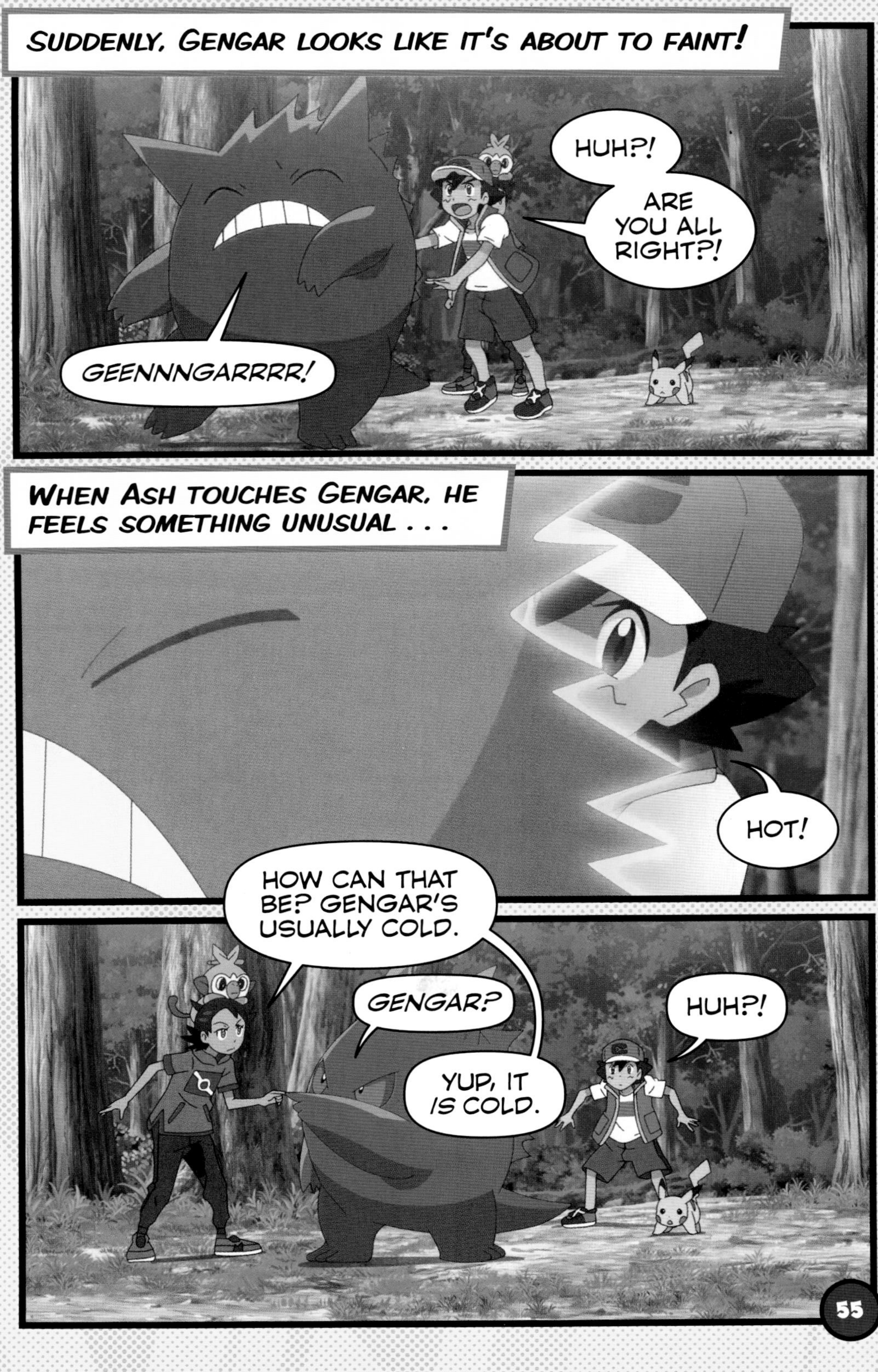
SUDDENLY, GENGAR LOOKS LIKE IT'S ABOUT TO FAINT!
HUH?!
ARE YOU ALL RIGHT?!
GEENNNGARRRR!
WHEN ASH TOUCHES GENGAR, HE FEELS SOMETHING UNUSUAL . . .
HOT!
HOW CAN THAT BE? GENGAR'S USUALLY COLD.
GENGAR?
YUP, IT IS COLD.
HUH?!

IN SINNOH, PAUL WAS KNOWN TO BE A BULLY. IT SEEMS LIKE MAYBE HE HASN'T CHANGED MUCH . . .

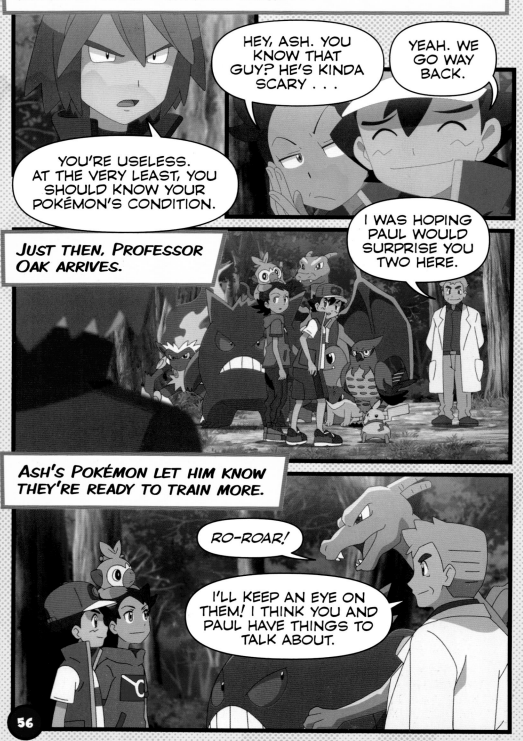

HEY, ASH. YOU KNOW THAT GUY? HE'S KINDA SCARY . . .

YEAH. WE GO WAY BACK.

YOU'RE USELESS. AT THE VERY LEAST, YOU SHOULD KNOW YOUR POKÉMON'S CONDITION.

I WAS HOPING PAUL WOULD SURPRISE YOU TWO HERE.

JUST THEN, PROFESSOR OAK ARRIVES.

ASH'S POKÉMON LET HIM KNOW THEY'RE READY TO TRAIN MORE.

RO-ROAR!

I'LL KEEP AN EYE ON THEM! I THINK YOU AND PAUL HAVE THINGS TO TALK ABOUT.

56

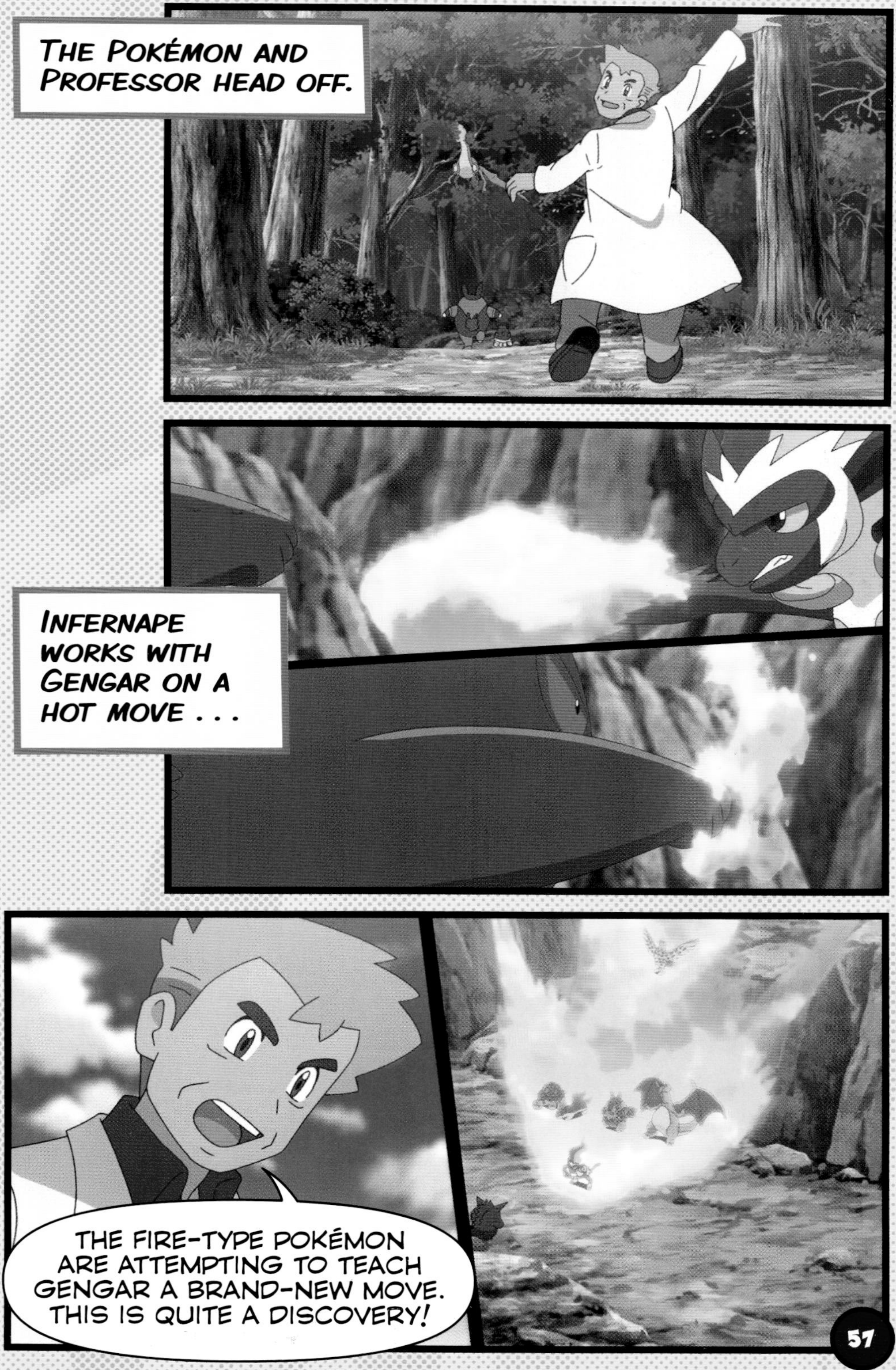
THE POKÉMON AND PROFESSOR HEAD OFF.
INFERNAPE WORKS WITH GENGAR ON A HOT MOVE . . .
THE FIRE-TYPE POKÉMON ARE ATTEMPTING TO TEACH GENGAR A BRAND-NEW MOVE. THIS IS QUITE A DISCOVERY!

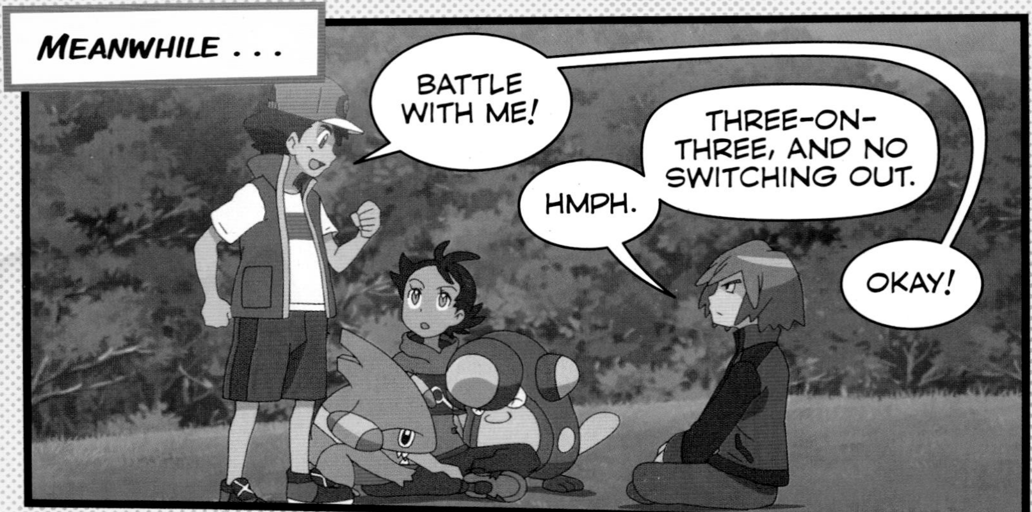
MEANWHILE . . .
BATTLE WITH ME!
HMPH.
THREE-ON-THREE, AND NO SWITCHING OUT.
OKAY!

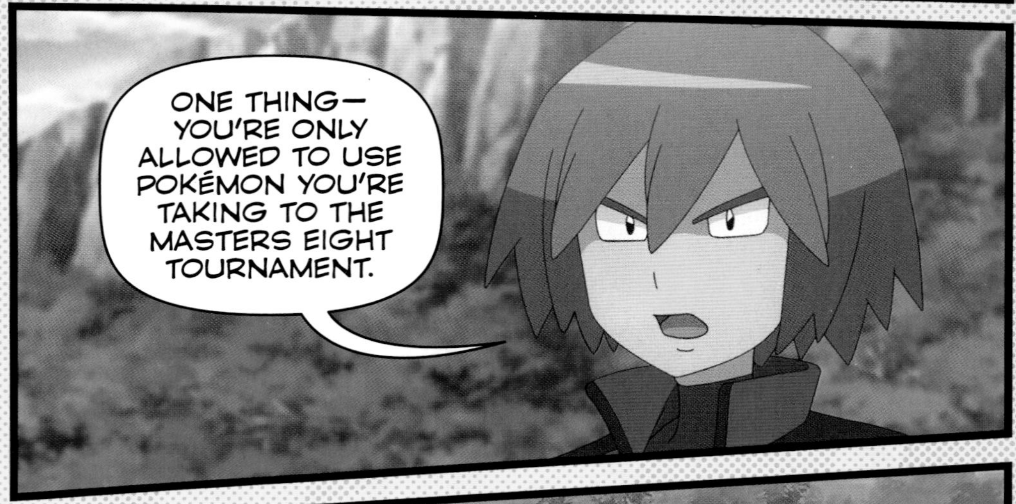
ONE THING—YOU'RE ONLY ALLOWED TO USE POKÉMON YOU'RE TAKING TO THE MASTERS EIGHT TOURNAMENT.

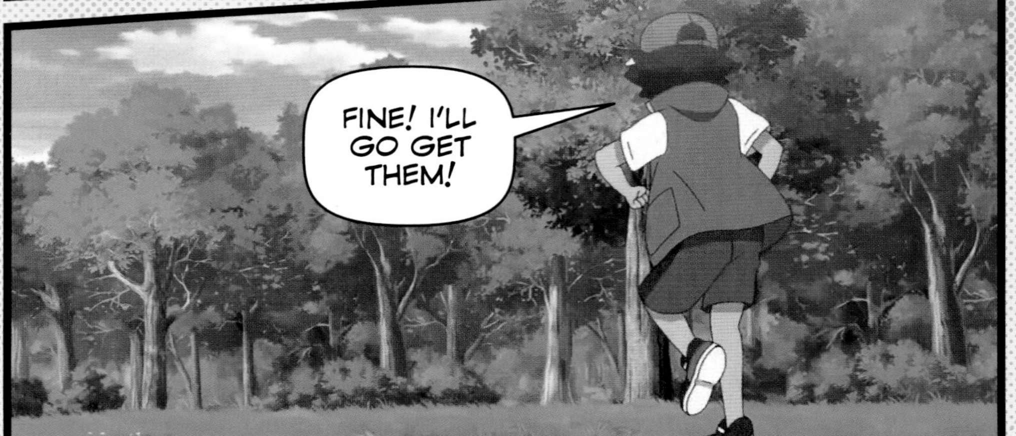
FINE! I'LL GO GET THEM!

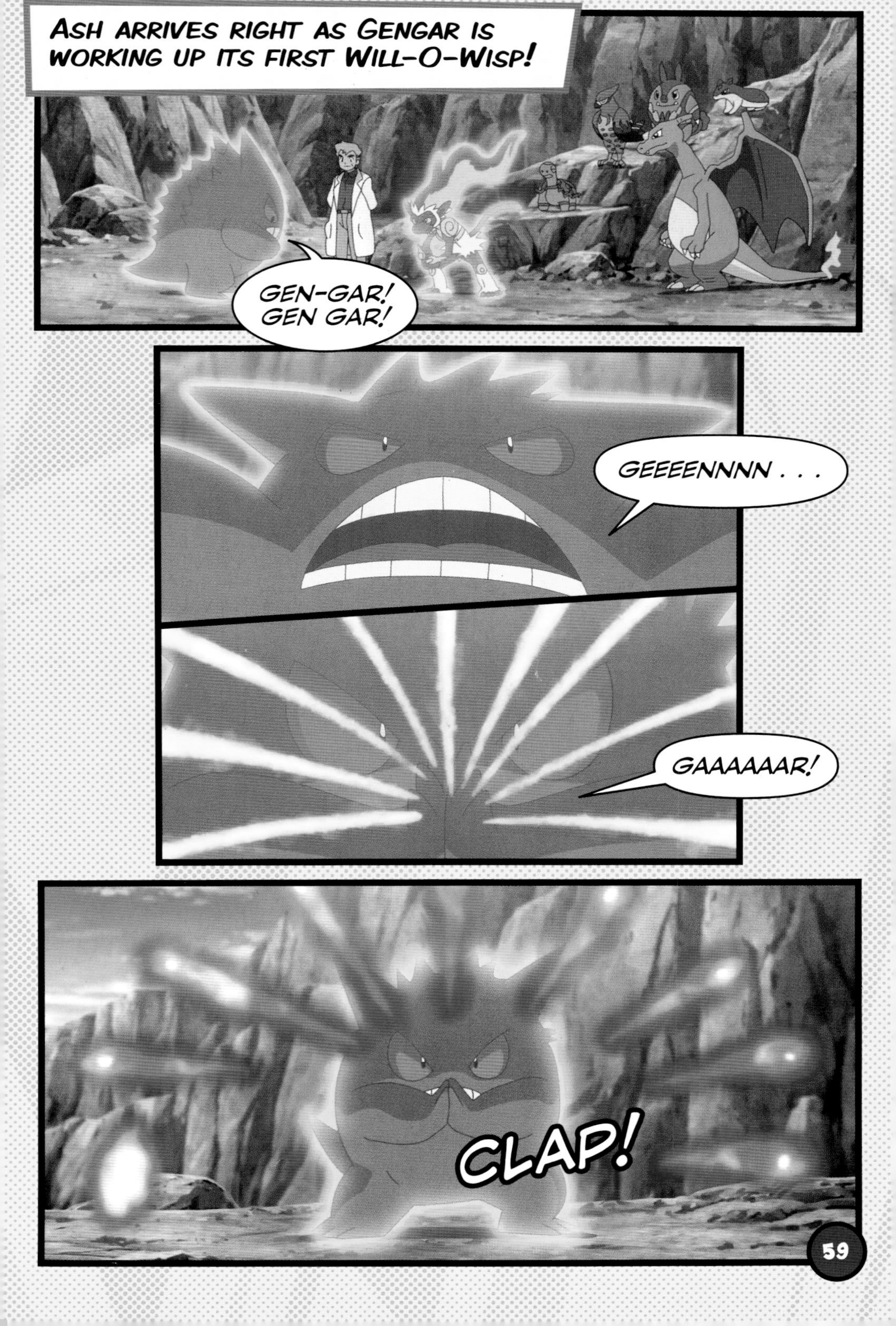
ASH ARRIVES RIGHT AS GENGAR IS WORKING UP ITS FIRST WILL-O-WISP!
GEN-GAR! GEN GAR!
GEEEENNNN . . .
GAAAAAAR!
CLAP!

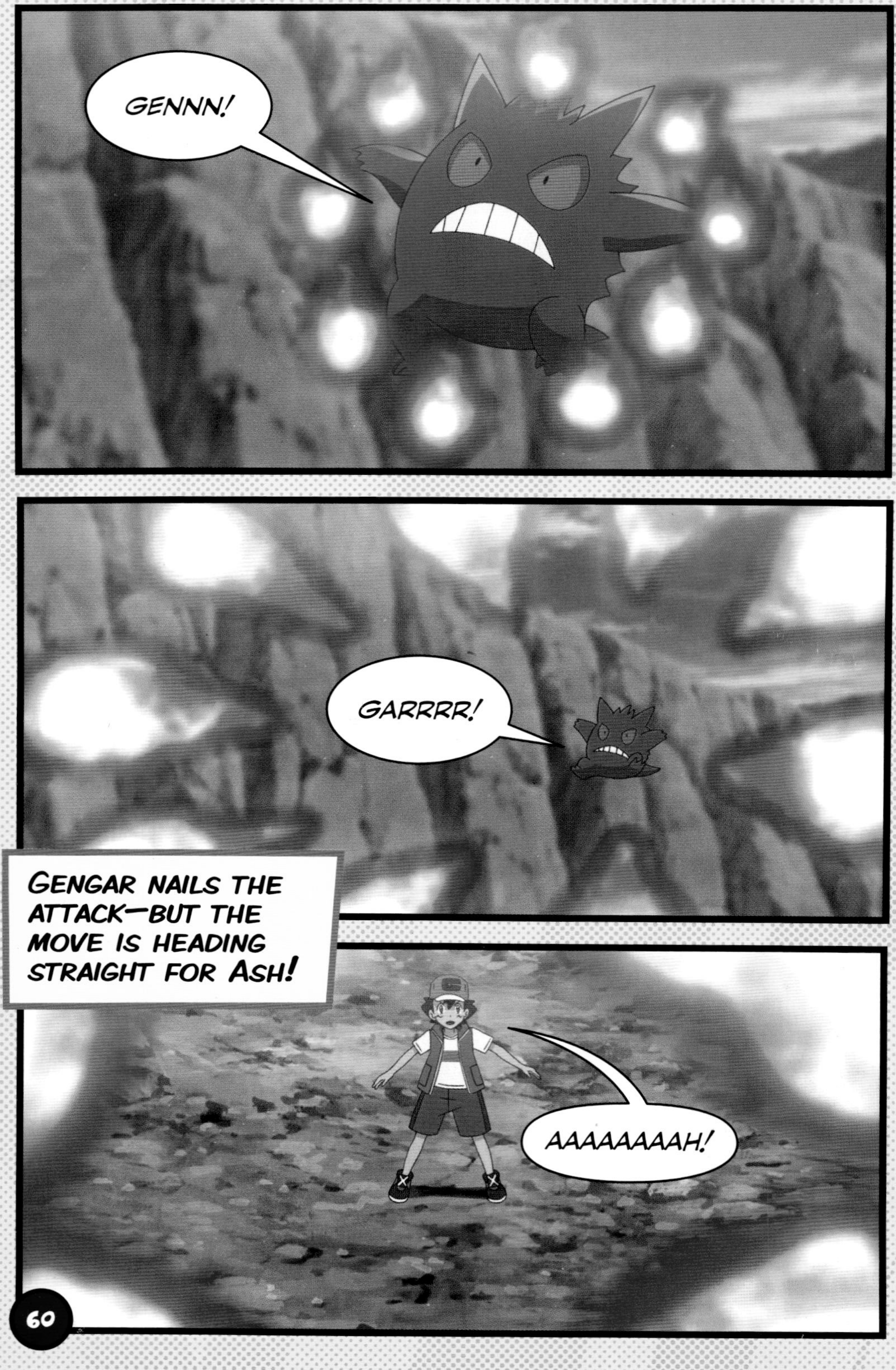
GENNN!
GARRRR!
GENGAR NAILS THE ATTACK—BUT THE MOVE IS HEADING STRAIGHT FOR ASH!
AAAAAAAAAH!

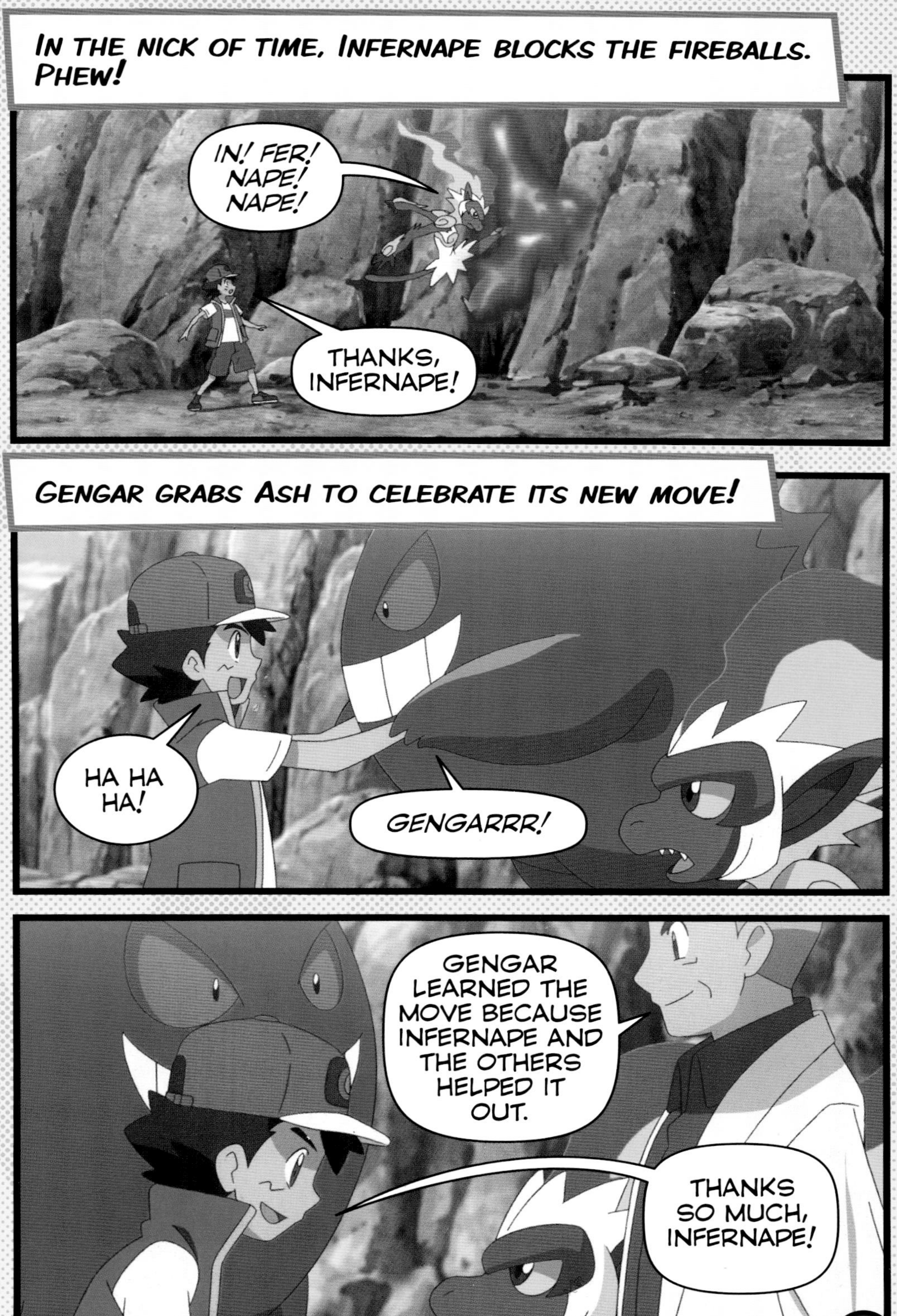
IN THE NICK OF TIME, INFERNAPE BLOCKS THE FIREBALLS. PHEW!
IN! FER! NAPE! NAPE!
THANKS, INFERNAPE!
GENGAR GRABS ASH TO CELEBRATE ITS NEW MOVE!
HA HA HA!
GENGARRR!
GENGAR LEARNED THE MOVE BECAUSE INFERNAPE AND THE OTHERS HELPED IT OUT.
THANKS SO MUCH, INFERNAPE!

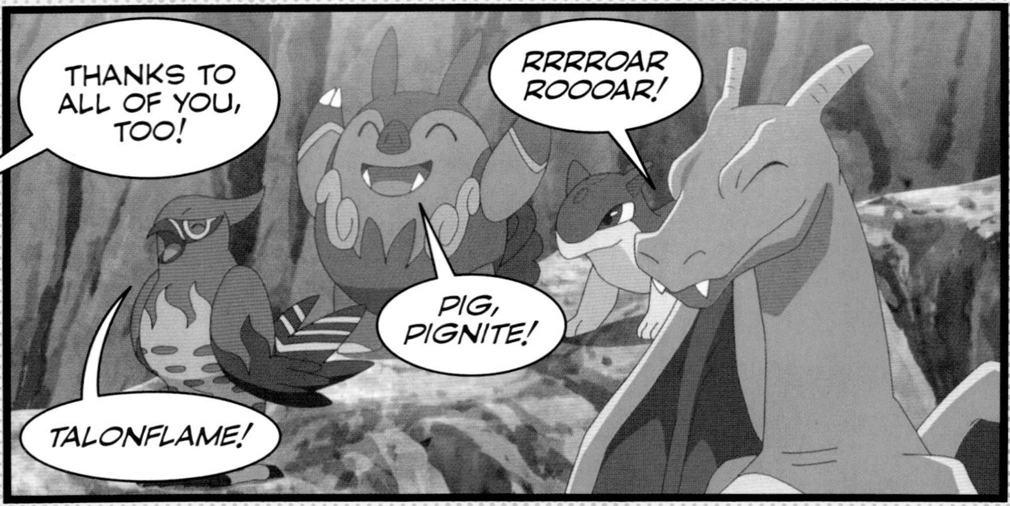
THANKS TO ALL OF YOU, TOO!
RRRROAR ROOOAR!
PIG, PIGNITE!
TALONFLAME!

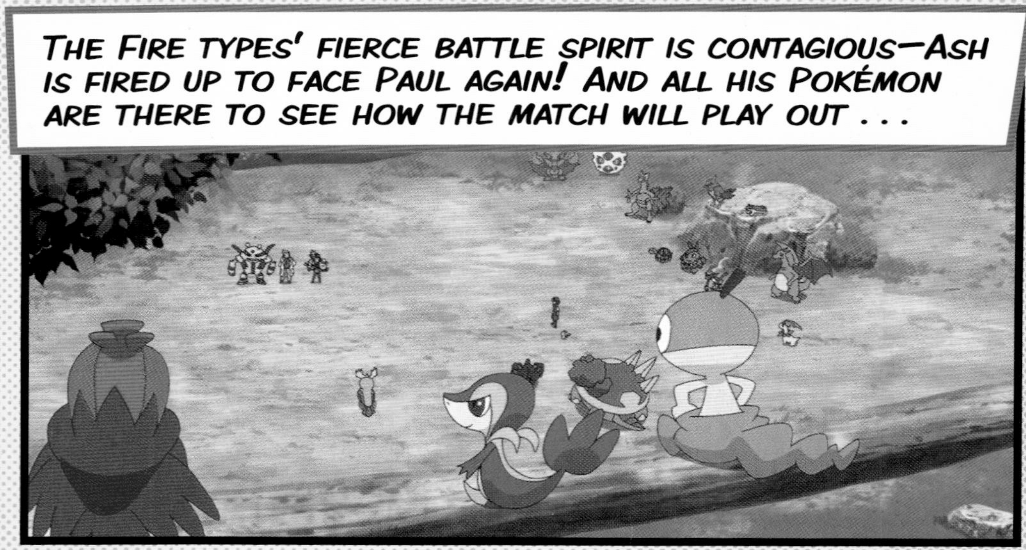
THE FIRE TYPES' FIERCE BATTLE SPIRIT IS CONTAGIOUS—ASH IS FIRED UP TO FACE PAUL AGAIN! AND ALL HIS POKÉMON ARE THERE TO SEE HOW THE MATCH WILL PLAY OUT . . .

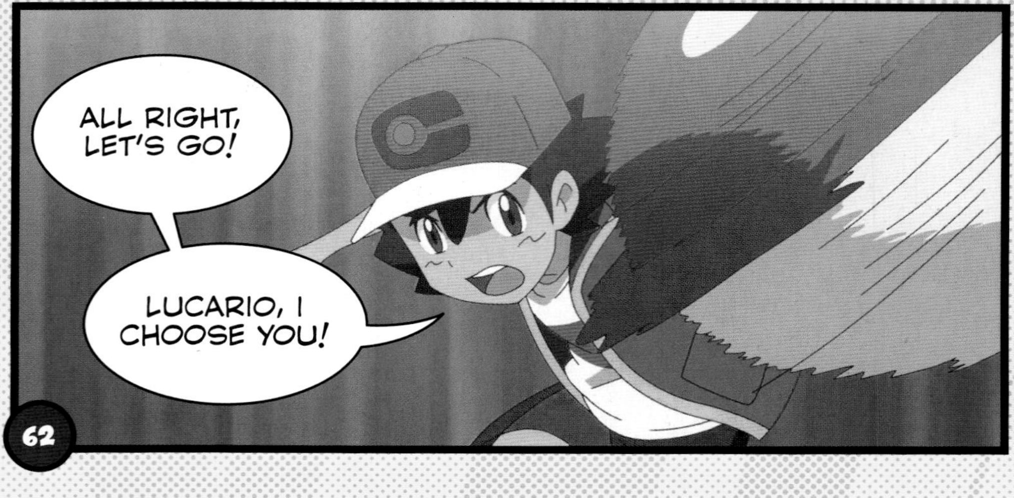
ALL RIGHT, LET'S GO!
LUCARIO, I CHOOSE YOU!

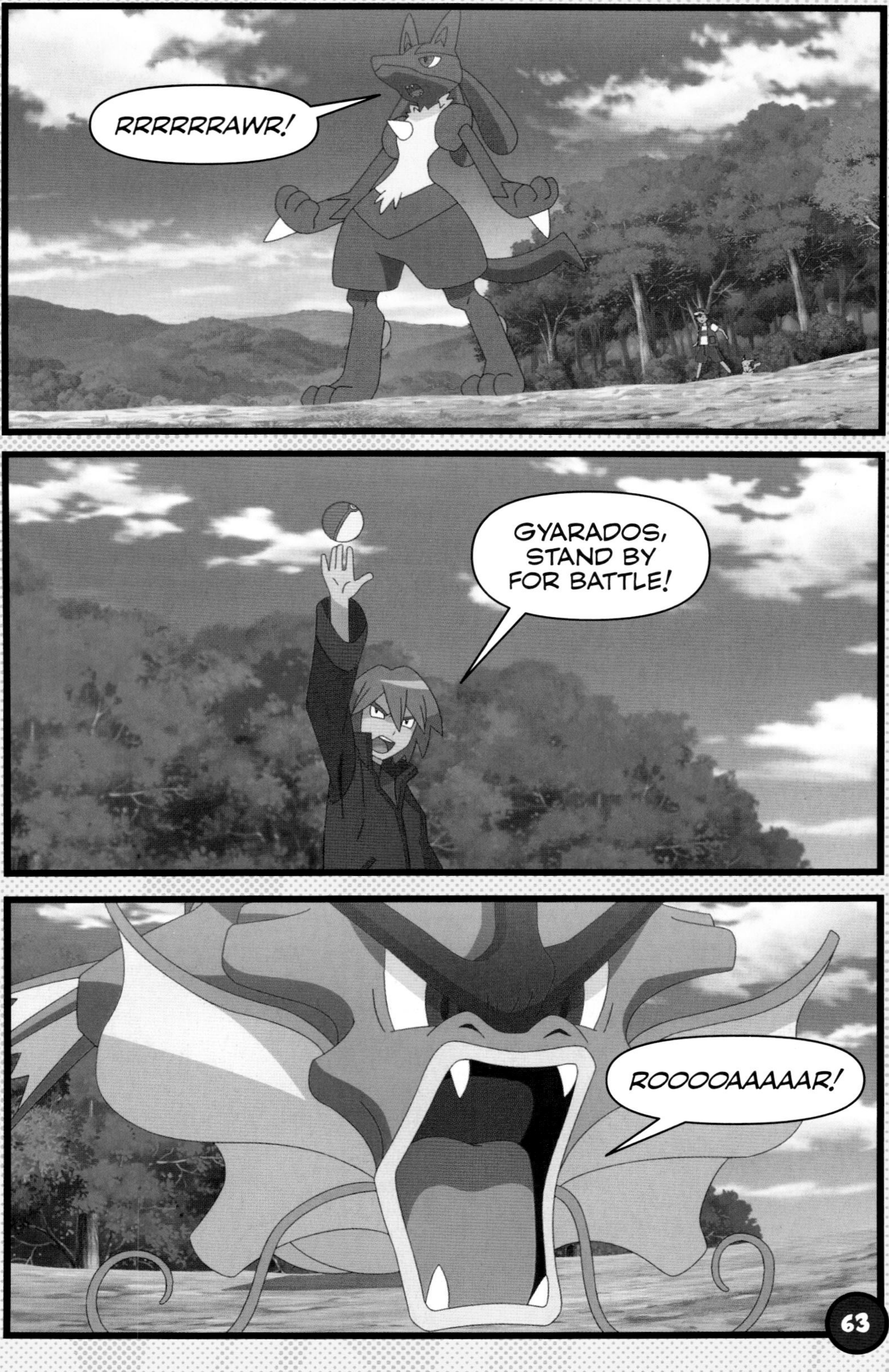
RRRRRRAWR!
GYARADOS, STAND BY FOR BATTLE!
ROOOOAAAAAR!

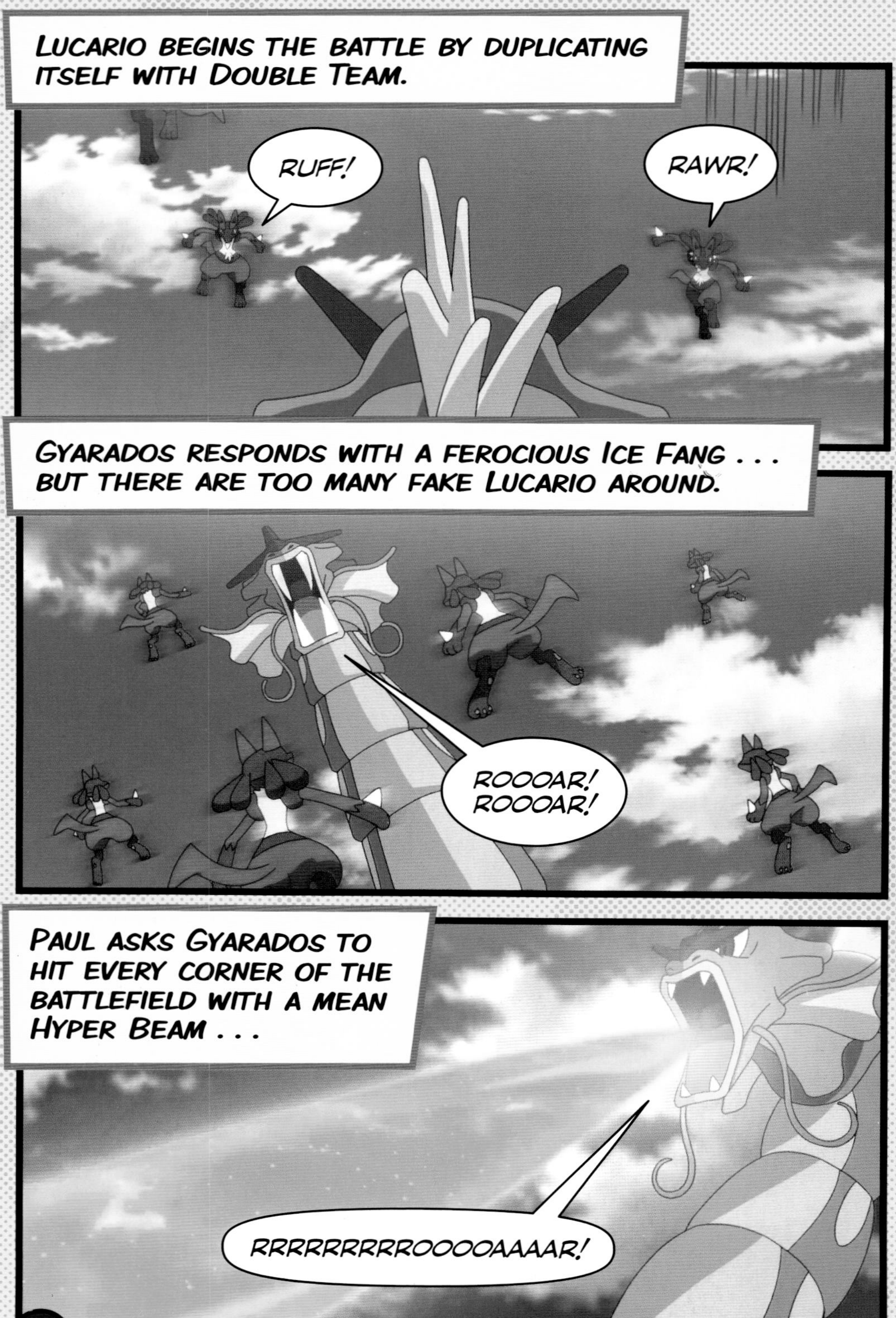
LUCARIO BEGINS THE BATTLE BY DUPLICATING ITSELF WITH DOUBLE TEAM.
RUFF!
RAWR!
GYARADOS RESPONDS WITH A FEROCIOUS ICE FANG . . . BUT THERE ARE TOO MANY FAKE LUCARIO AROUND.
ROOOAR! ROOOAR!
PAUL ASKS GYARADOS TO HIT EVERY CORNER OF THE BATTLEFIELD WITH A MEAN HYPER BEAM . . .
RRRRRRRRROOOOAAAAR!

As the move spins around the battlefield, Gyarados destroys Lucario's Double Team dupes.
POW!
POW!
POW!
But the real Lucario still has the element of surprise on its side . . .
RAWR!
Lucario lunges with a powerful ball of Aura Sphere ready!
RAAAAAAAAWW!

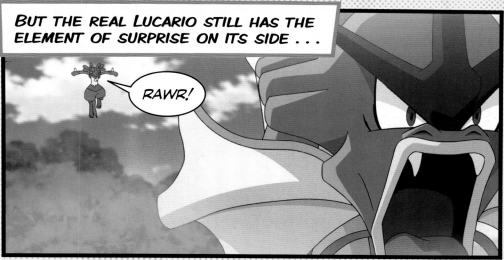

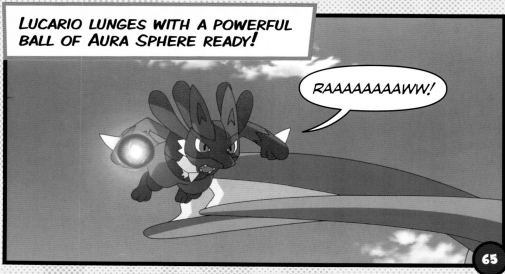

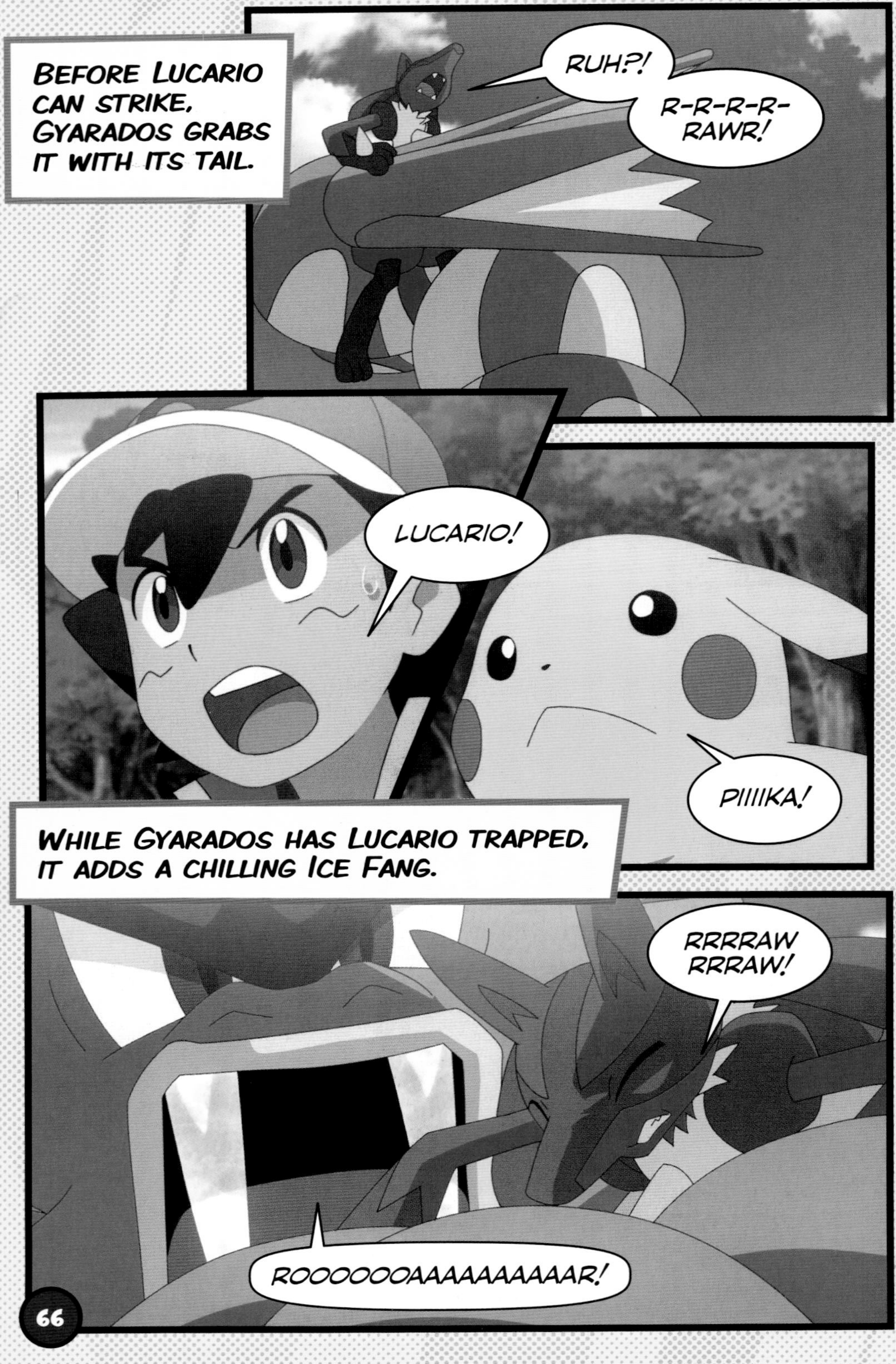
BEFORE LUCARIO CAN STRIKE, GYARADOS GRABS IT WITH ITS TAIL.
RUH?!
R-R-R-R-RAWR!
LUCARIO!
PIIIIKA!
WHILE GYARADOS HAS LUCARIO TRAPPED, IT ADDS A CHILLING ICE FANG.
RRRRAW RRRAW!
ROOOOOOAAAAAAAAAAR!

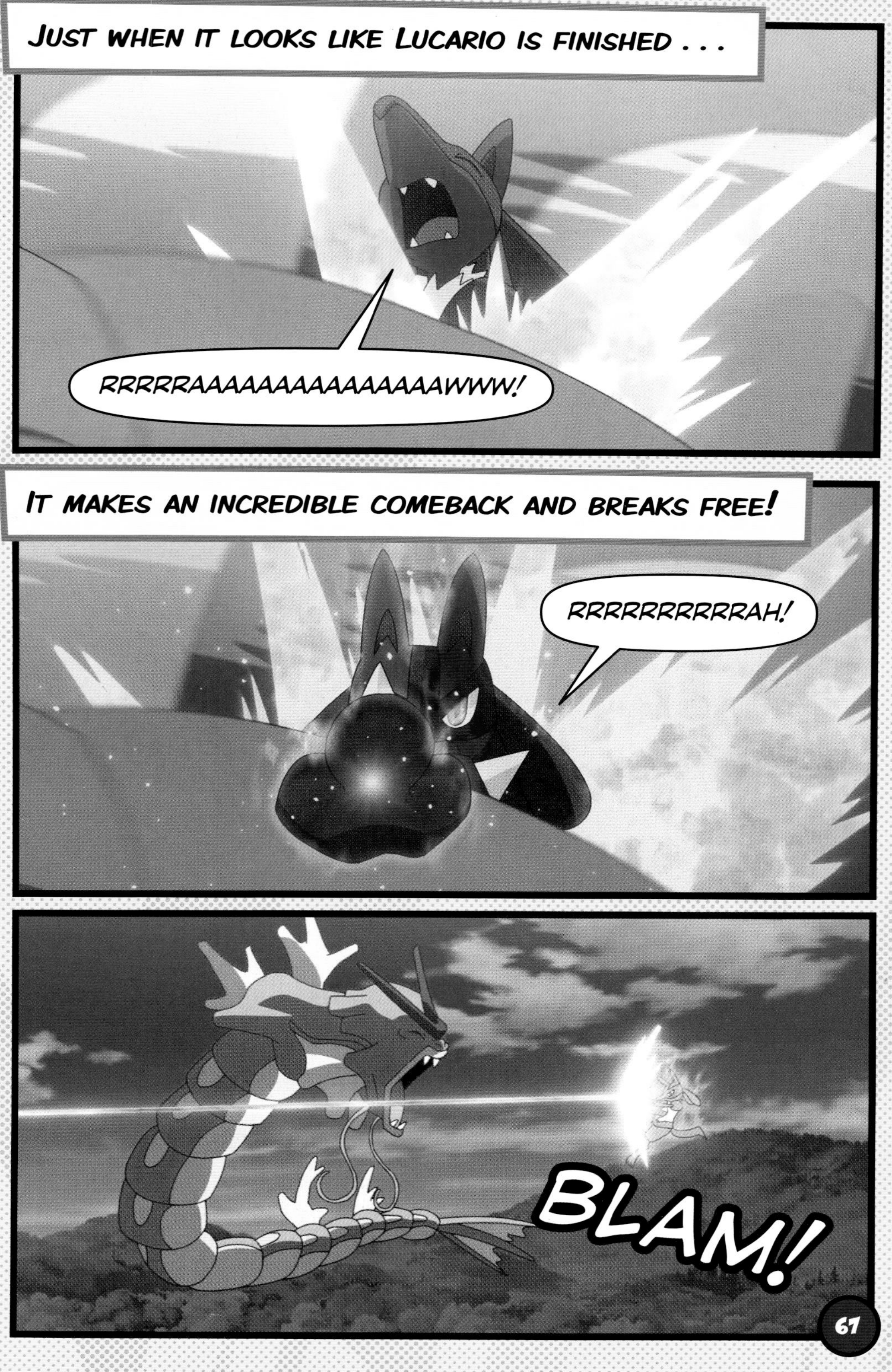

JUST WHEN IT LOOKS LIKE LUCARIO IS FINISHED . . .
RRRRRAAAAAAAAAAAAAAAAAWWW!
IT MAKES AN INCREDIBLE COMEBACK AND BREAKS FREE!
RRRRRRRRRRRAH!
BLAM!

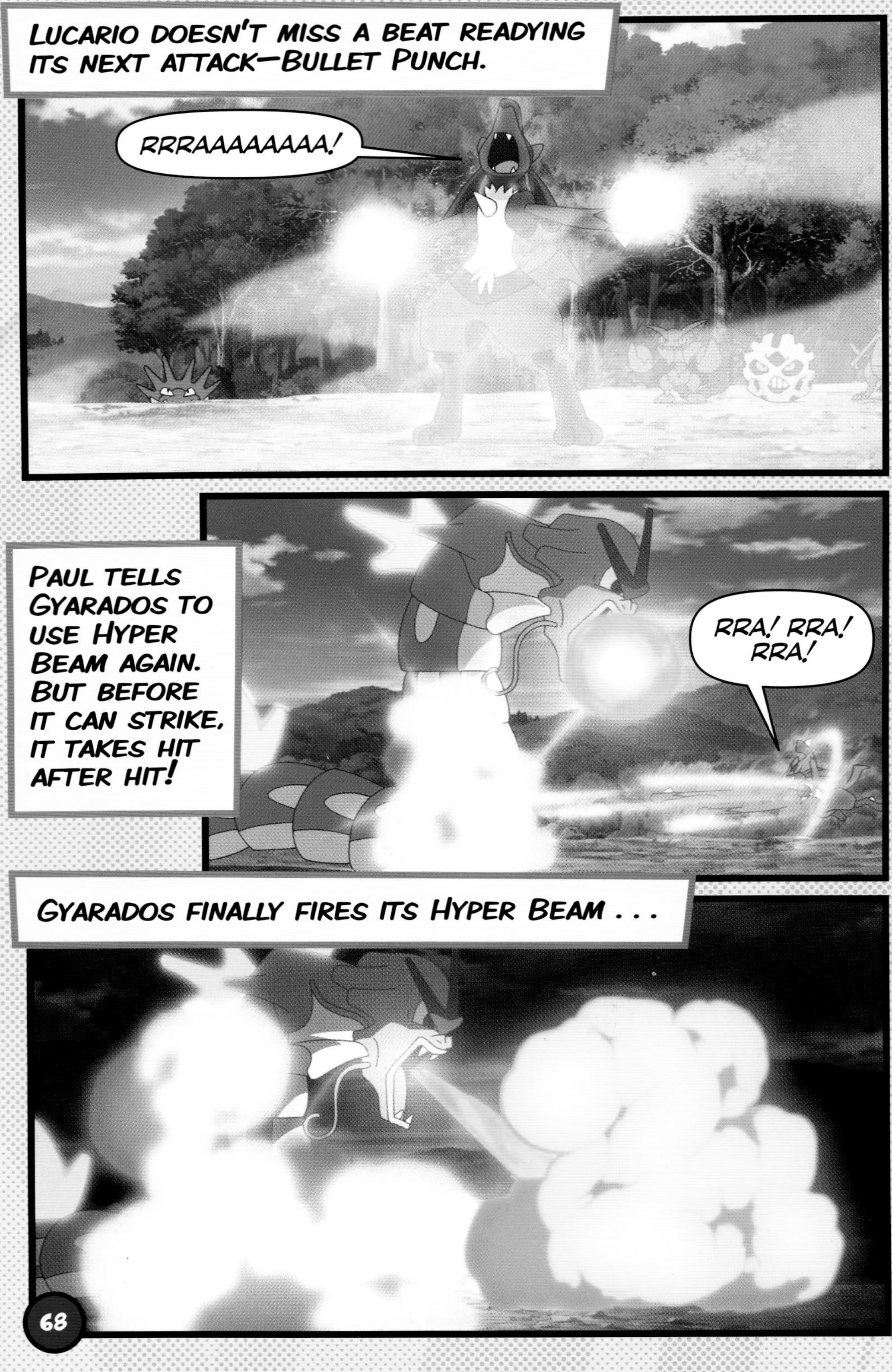
Lucario doesn't miss a beat readying its next attack—Bullet Punch.
RRRAAAAAAAAA!
Paul tells Gyarados to use Hyper Beam again. But before it can strike, it takes hit after hit!
RRA! RRA! RRA!
Gyarados finally fires its Hyper Beam . . .

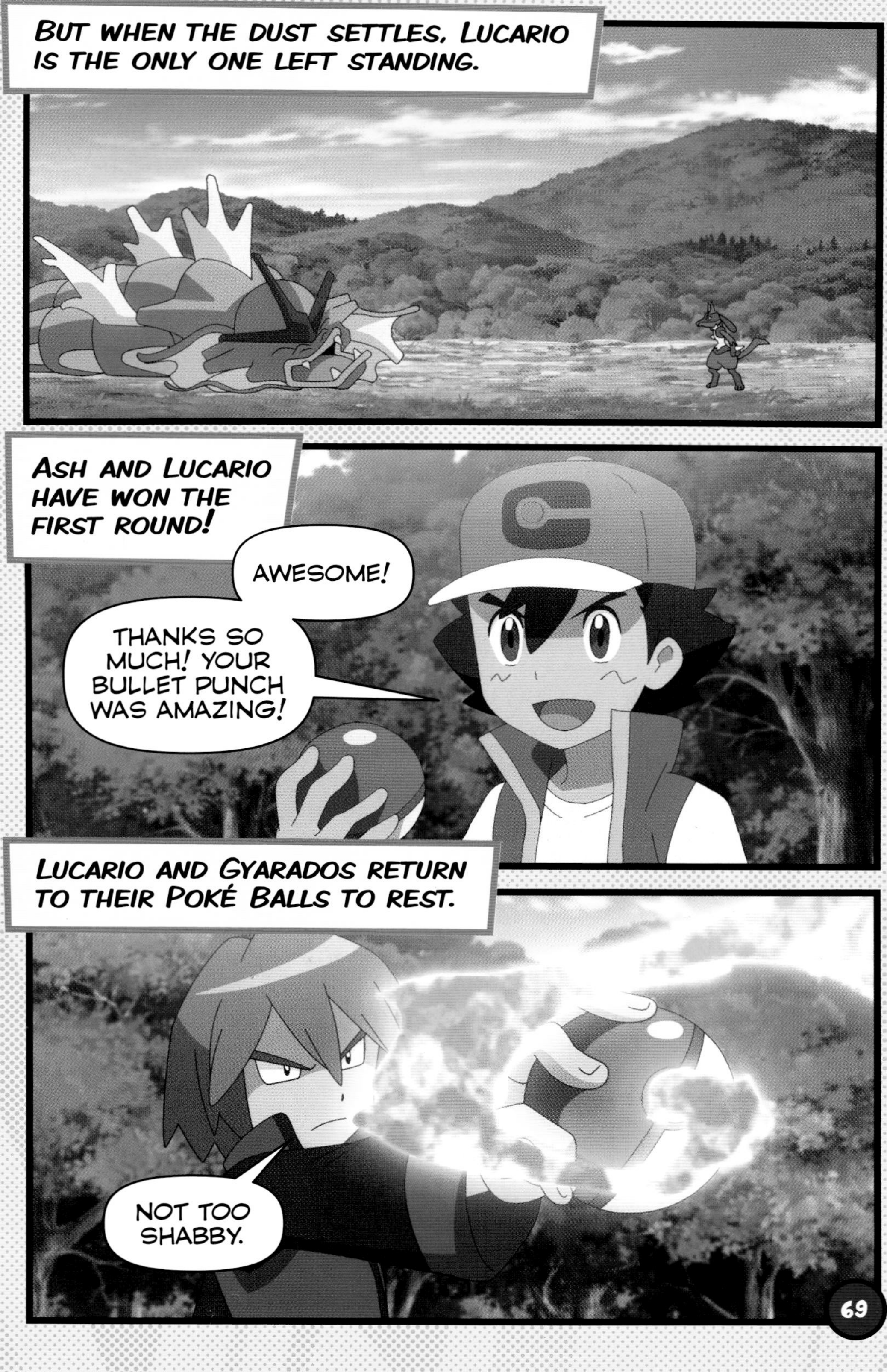
BUT WHEN THE DUST SETTLES, LUCARIO IS THE ONLY ONE LEFT STANDING.
ASH AND LUCARIO HAVE WON THE FIRST ROUND!
AWESOME!
THANKS SO MUCH! YOUR BULLET PUNCH WAS AMAZING!
LUCARIO AND GYARADOS RETURN TO THEIR POKÉ BALLS TO REST.
NOT TOO SHABBY.

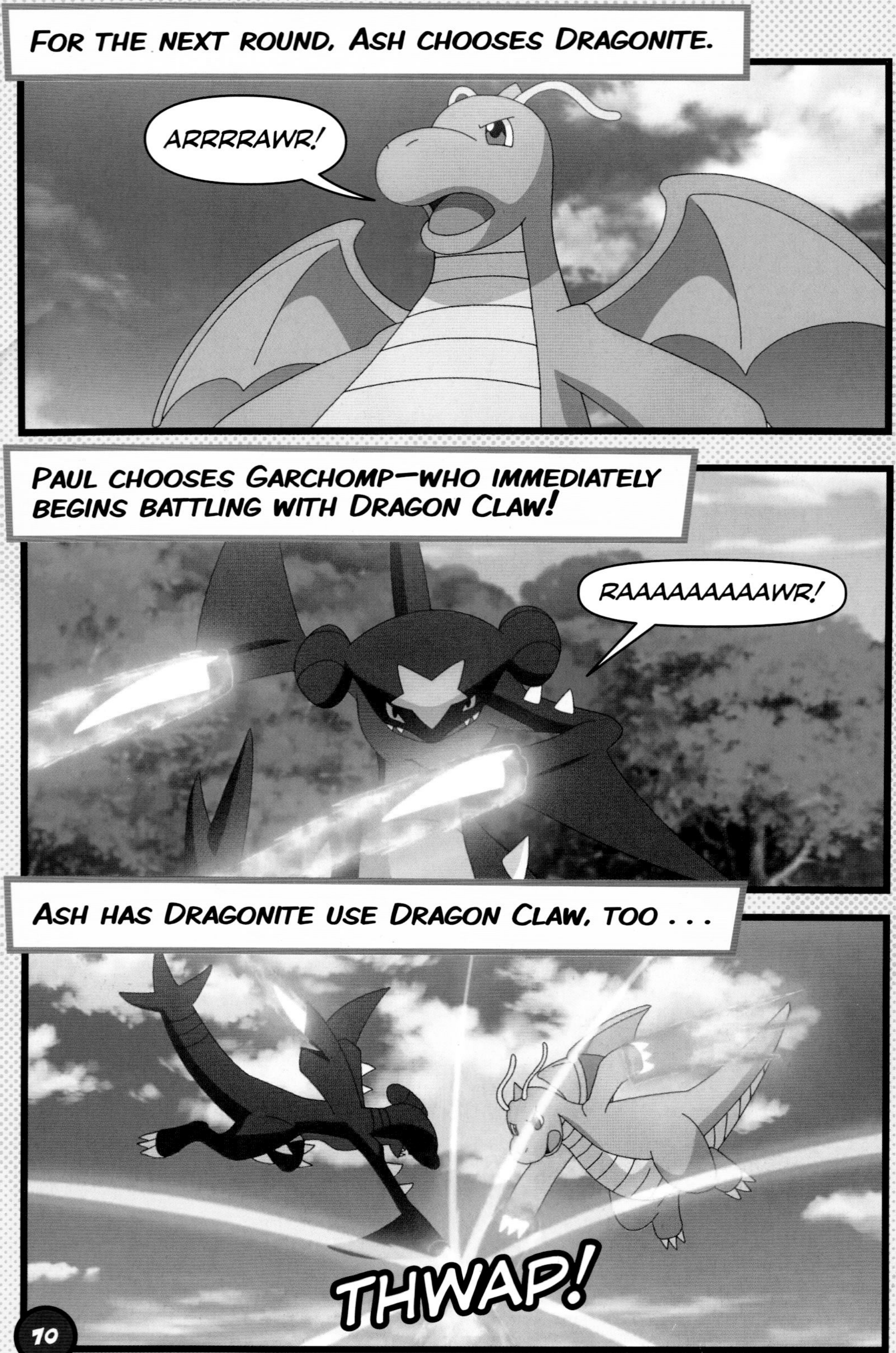
For the next round, Ash chooses Dragonite.
ARRRRAWR!
Paul chooses Garchomp—who immediately begins battling with Dragon Claw!
RAAAAAAAAAWR!
Ash has Dragonite use Dragon Claw, too . . .
THWAP!

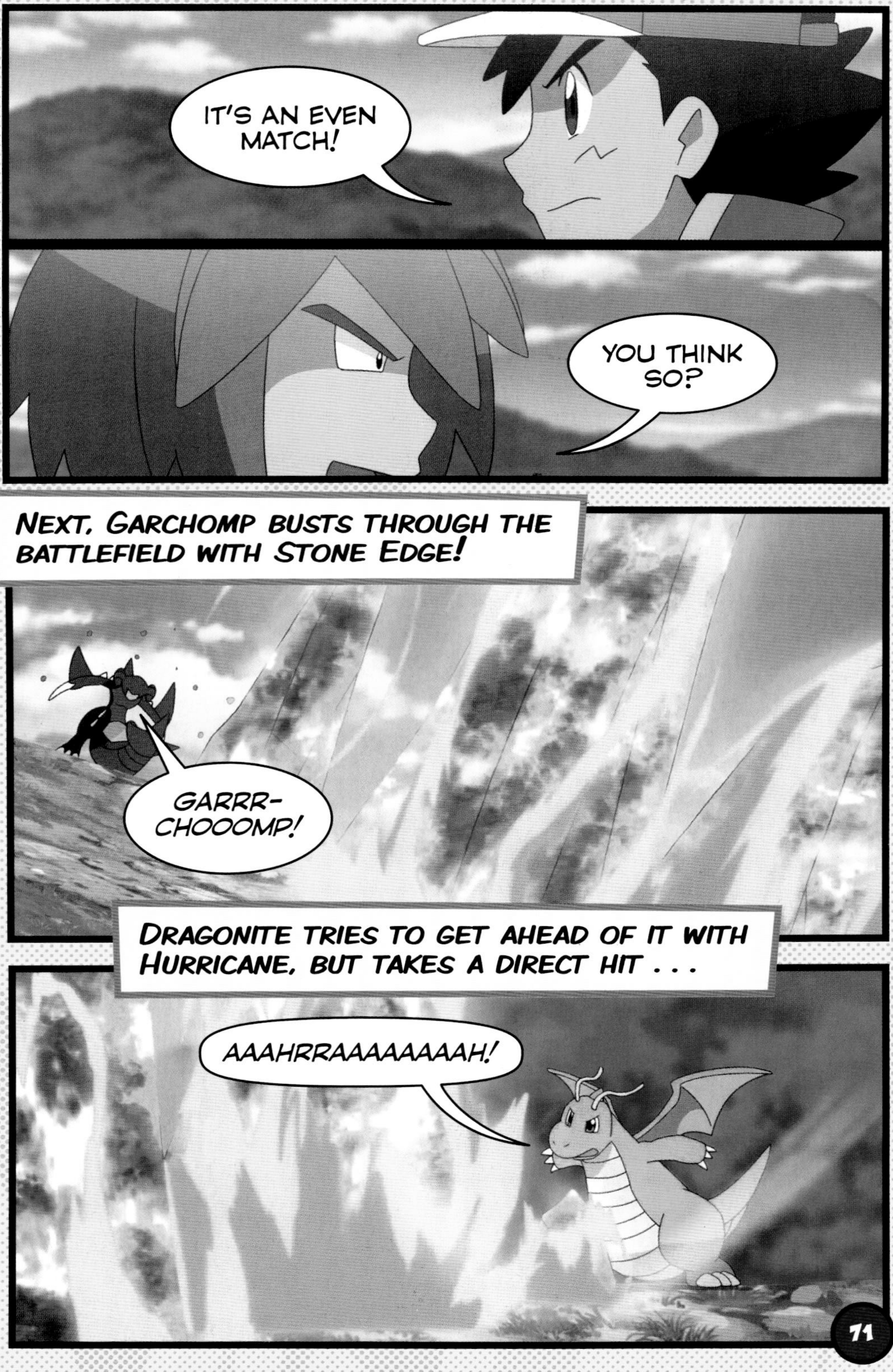
IT'S AN EVEN MATCH!
YOU THINK SO?
NEXT, GARCHOMP BUSTS THROUGH THE BATTLEFIELD WITH STONE EDGE!
GARRR-CHOOOMP!
DRAGONITE TRIES TO GET AHEAD OF IT WITH HURRICANE, BUT TAKES A DIRECT HIT . . .
AAAHRRAAAAAAAAAH!

GARCHOMP'S NEXT MOVE IS DRACO METEOR.

GARRRRRR!

ASH HAS DRAGONITE PREPARE DRACO METEOR, TOO . . .

DRRRRAAAAAAAAAA!

BUT IT'S NOT JUST ANY DRACO METEOR—ASH PUTS HIS OWN TWIST ON THE MOVE, WHICH HE CALLS *DRAGONITE METEOR!*

NOW, FOLLOW THE DRACO METEOR AND THEN ATTACK!

DRAAAAAAAA!

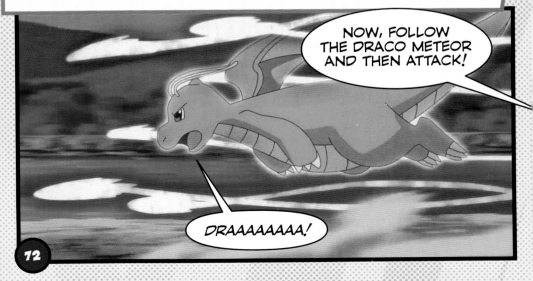

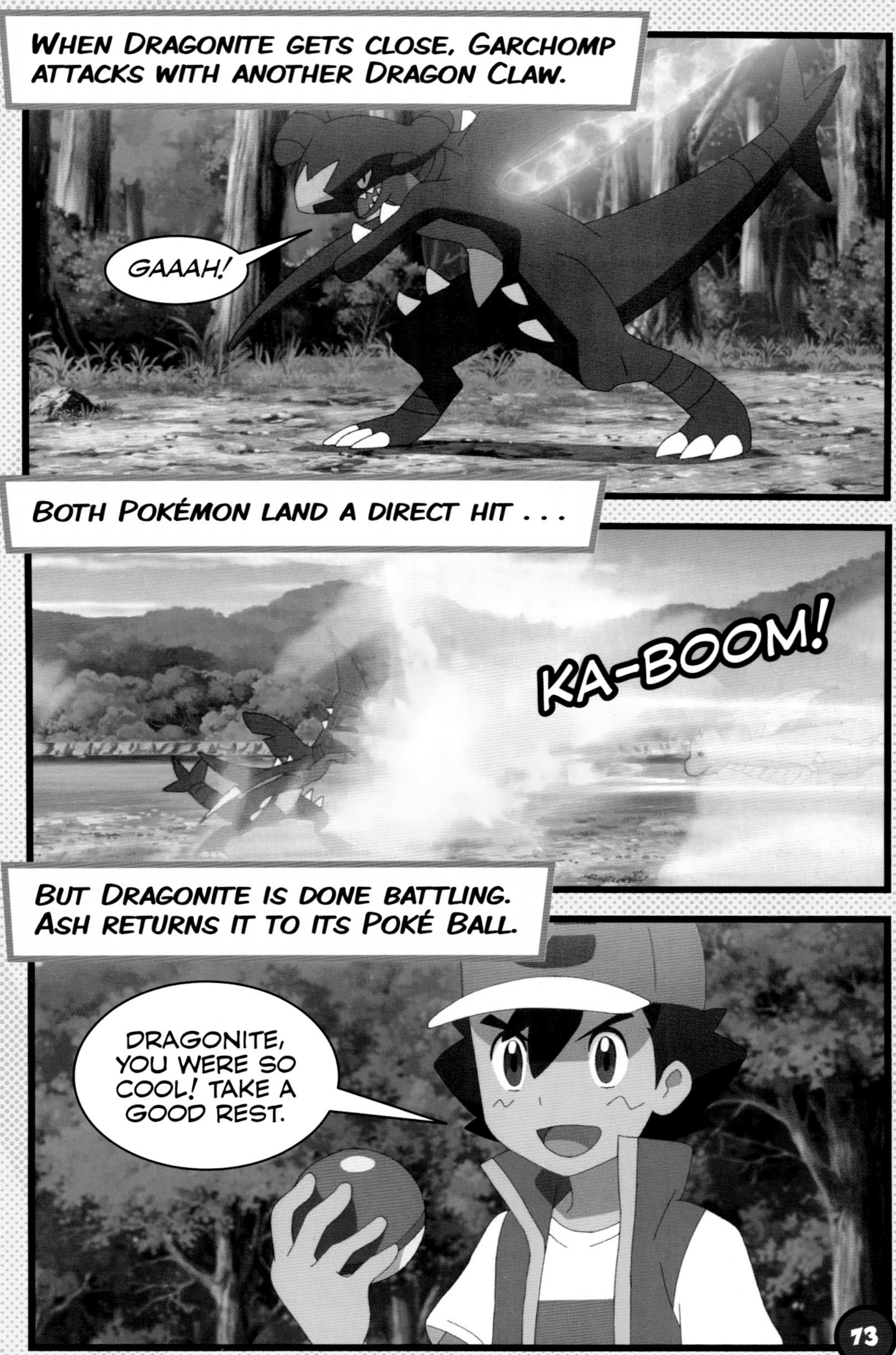
WHEN DRAGONITE GETS CLOSE, GARCHOMP ATTACKS WITH ANOTHER DRAGON CLAW.
GAAAH!
BOTH POKÉMON LAND A DIRECT HIT . . .
KA-BOOM!
BUT DRAGONITE IS DONE BATTLING. ASH RETURNS IT TO ITS POKÉ BALL.
DRAGONITE, YOU WERE SO COOL! TAKE A GOOD REST.

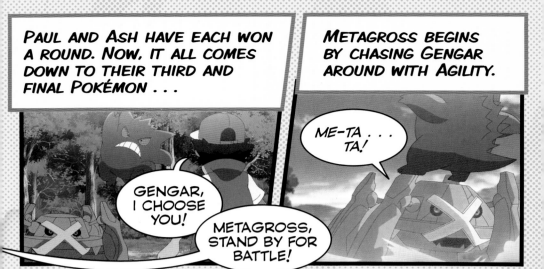

PAUL AND ASH HAVE EACH WON A ROUND. NOW, IT ALL COMES DOWN TO THEIR THIRD AND FINAL POKÉMON . . .

METAGROSS BEGINS BY CHASING GENGAR AROUND WITH AGILITY.

ME-TA . . . TA!

GENGAR, I CHOOSE YOU!

METAGROSS, STAND BY FOR BATTLE!

METAGROSS GETS CLOSE, BUT GENGAR IS GREAT AT DODGING!

GEN-GAR GEN-GAR!

GENGAR RESPONDS WITH SHADOW BALL . . .

GENGAAARRR!

BUT METAGROSS IS GREAT AT DODGING, TOO.

NEXT, METAGROSS USES PSYCHIC.

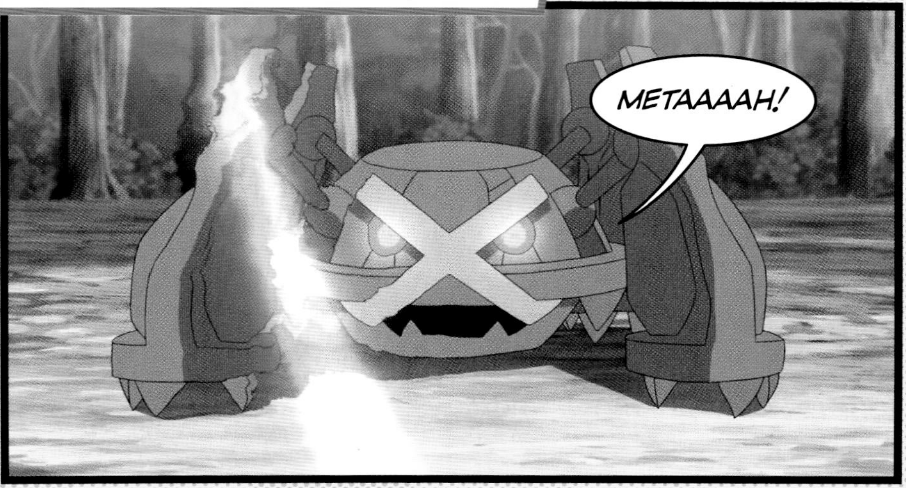
METAAAAH!

UNDER ITS CONTROL, GENGAR IS EVEN SILLIER THAN USUAL . . .

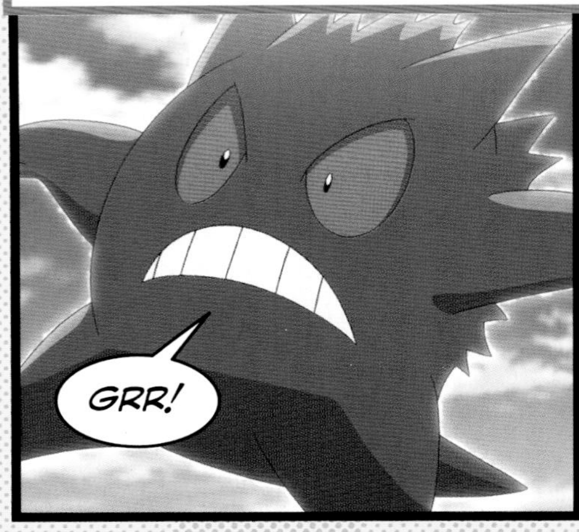
GRR!

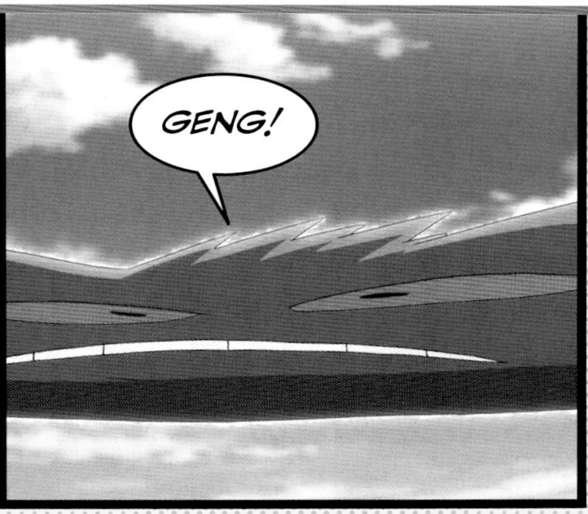
GENG!

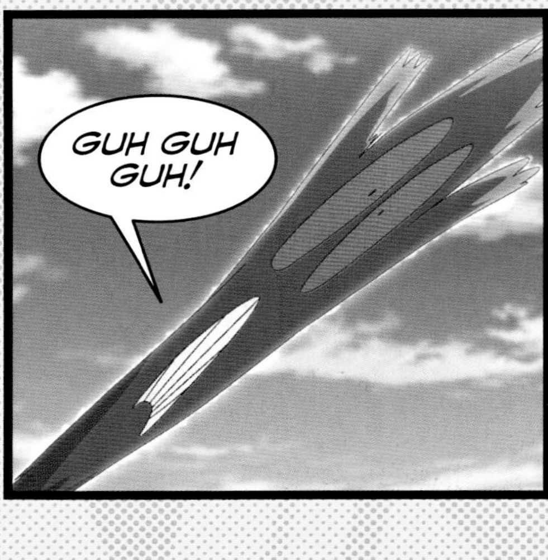
GUH GUH
GUH!

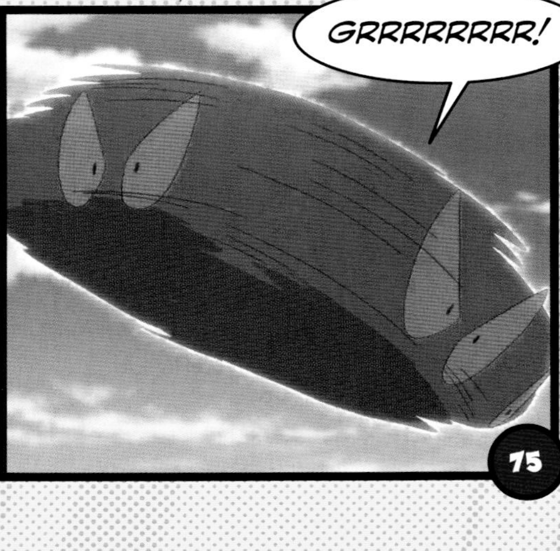
GRRRRRRRR!

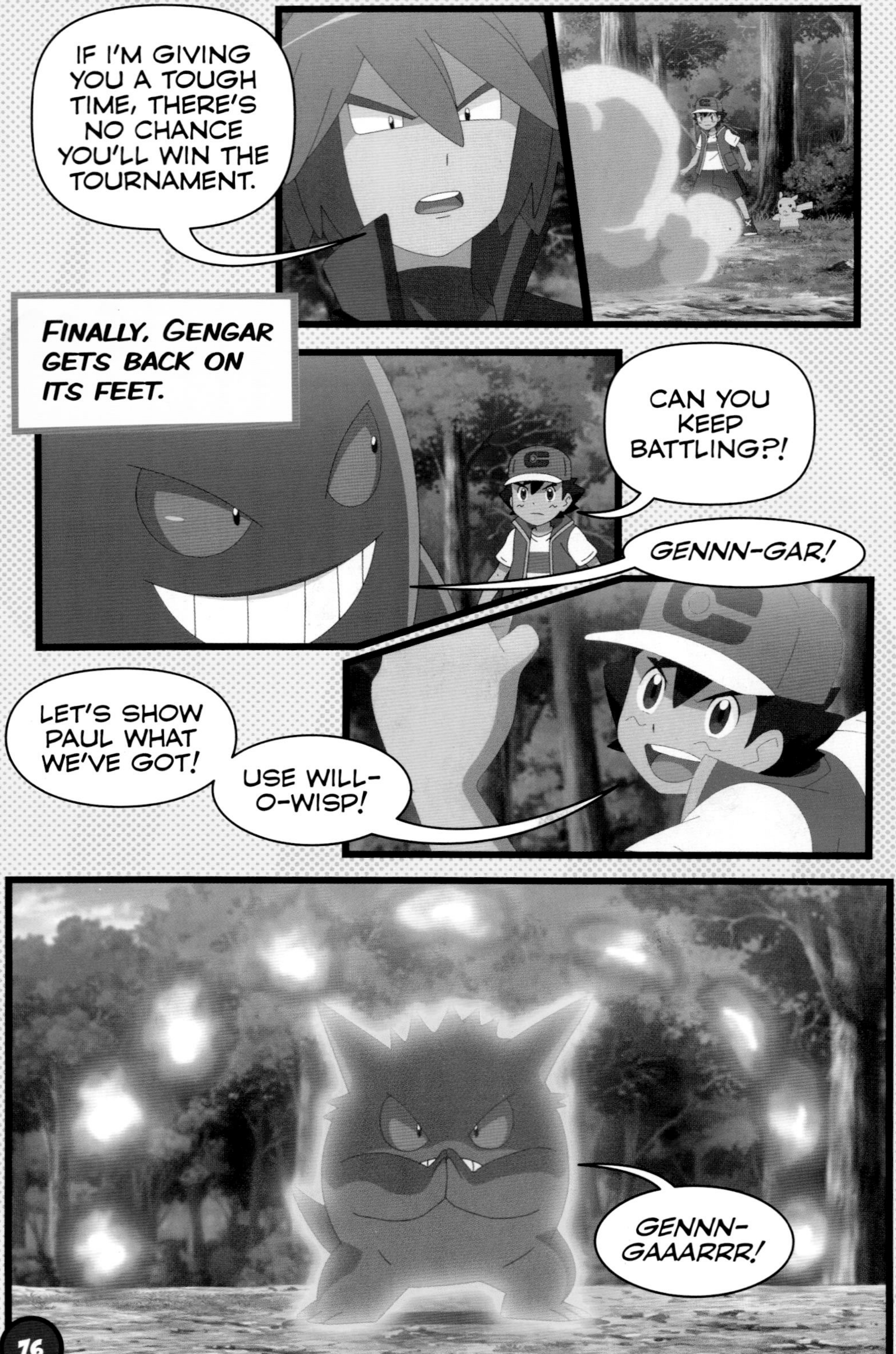
IF I'M GIVING YOU A TOUGH TIME, THERE'S NO CHANCE YOU'LL WIN THE TOURNAMENT.
FINALLY, GENGAR GETS BACK ON ITS FEET.
CAN YOU KEEP BATTLING?!
GENNN-GAR!
LET'S SHOW PAUL WHAT WE'VE GOT!
USE WILL-O-WISP!
GENNN-GAAARRR!

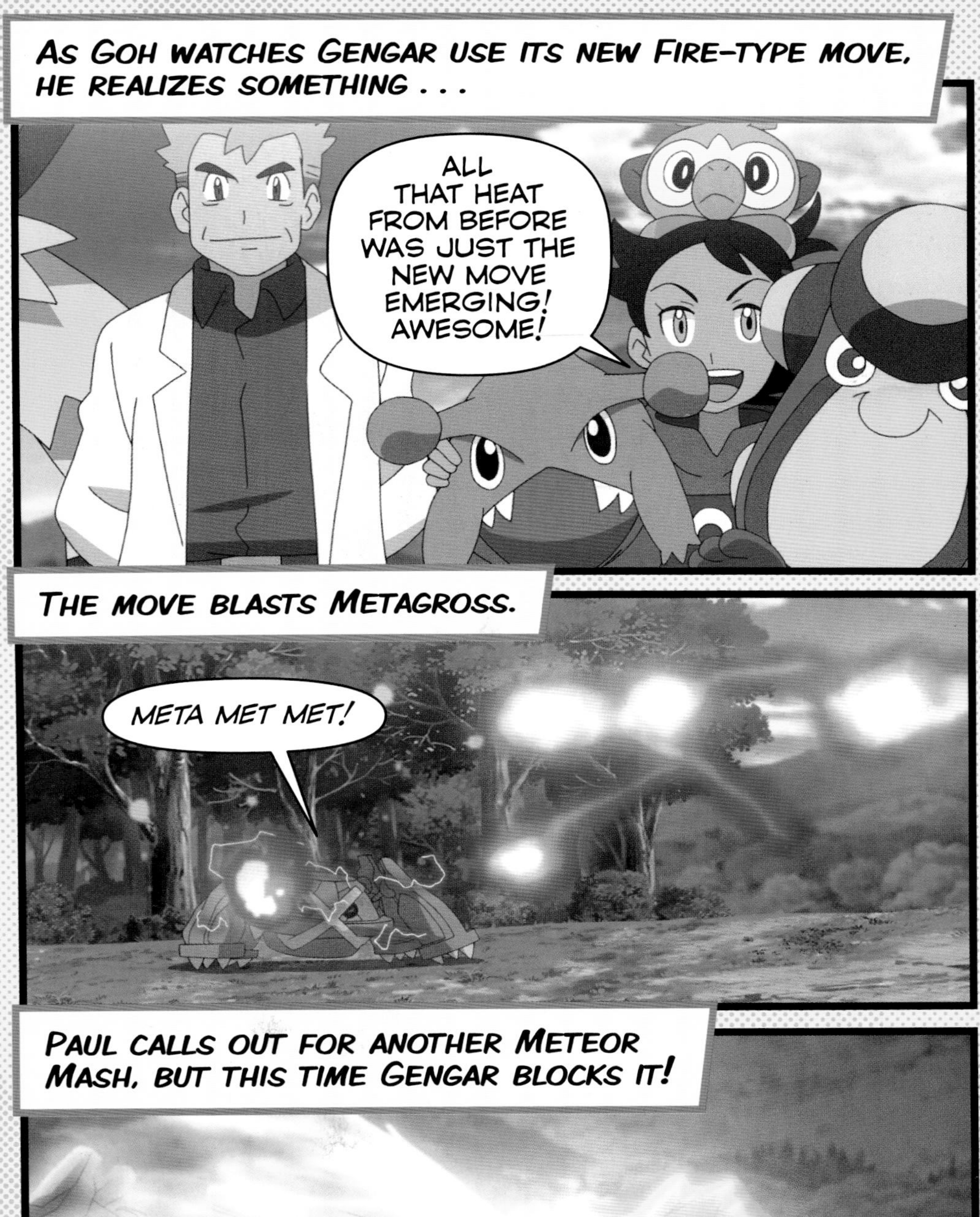
As Goh watches Gengar use its new Fire-type move, he realizes something . . .
ALL THAT HEAT FROM BEFORE WAS JUST THE NEW MOVE EMERGING! AWESOME!
The move blasts Metagross.
META MET MET!
Paul calls out for another Meteor Mash, but this time Gengar blocks it!
MET . . . TA . . . GROSS . . .

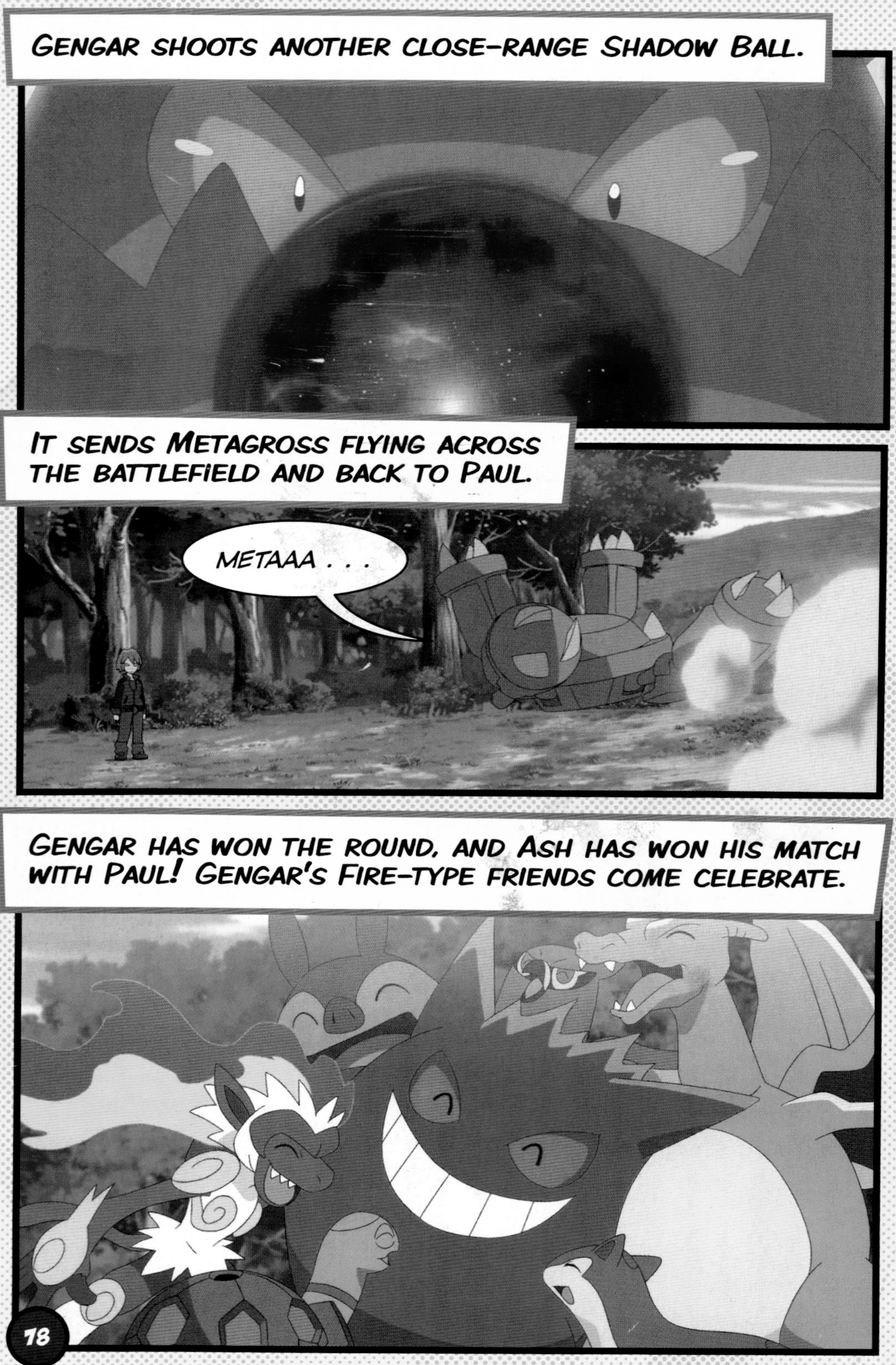
GENGAR SHOOTS ANOTHER CLOSE-RANGE SHADOW BALL.
IT SENDS METAGROSS FLYING ACROSS THE BATTLEFIELD AND BACK TO PAUL.
METAAA . . .
GENGAR HAS WON THE ROUND, AND ASH HAS WON HIS MATCH WITH PAUL! GENGAR'S FIRE-TYPE FRIENDS COME CELEBRATE.

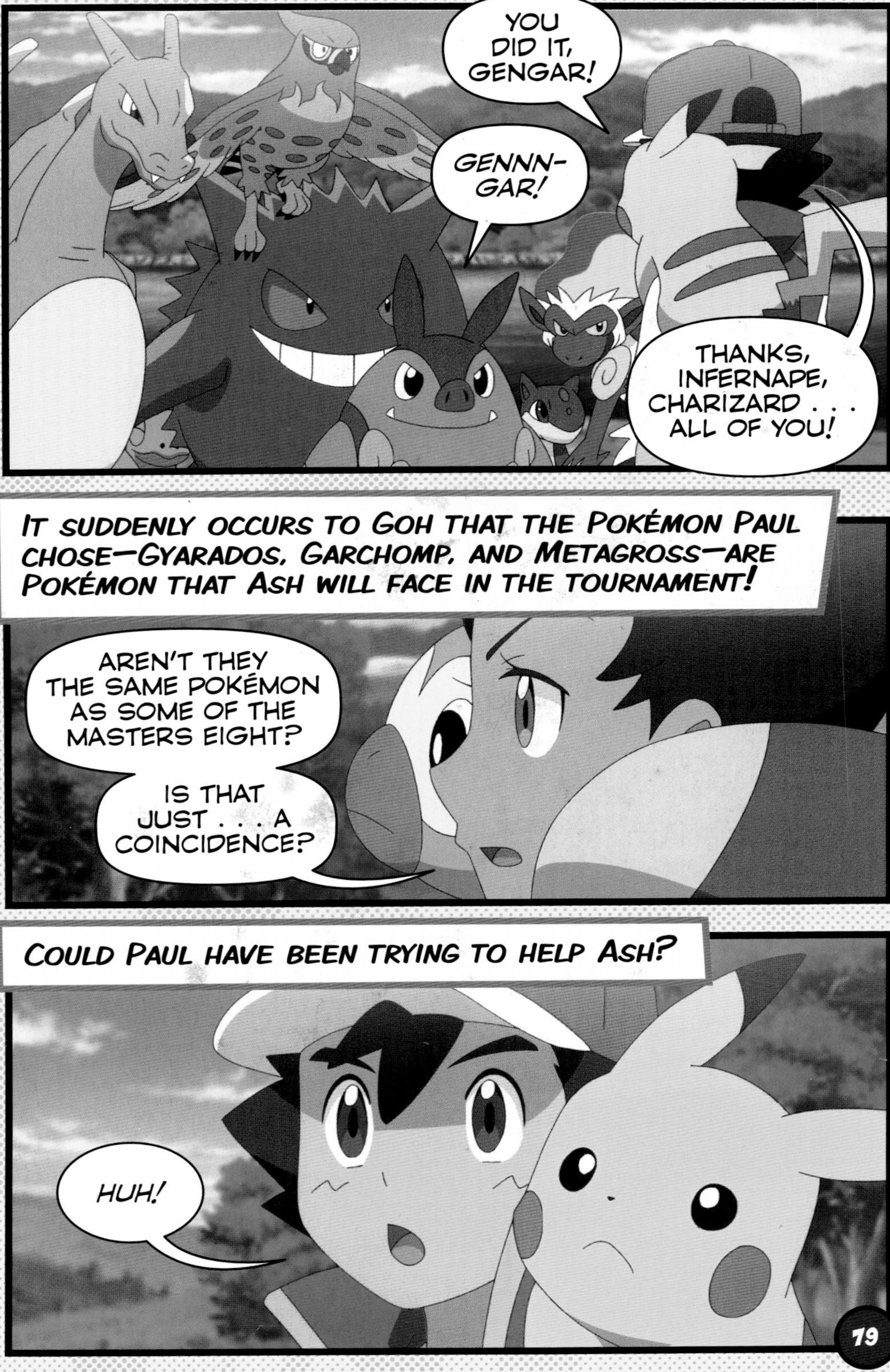
YOU DID IT, GENGAR!
GENNN-GAR!
THANKS, INFERNAPE, CHARIZARD . . . ALL OF YOU!
IT SUDDENLY OCCURS TO GOH THAT THE POKÉMON PAUL CHOSE—GYARADOS, GARCHOMP, AND METAGROSS—ARE POKÉMON THAT ASH WILL FACE IN THE TOURNAMENT!
AREN'T THEY THE SAME POKÉMON AS SOME OF THE MASTERS EIGHT?
IS THAT JUST . . . A COINCIDENCE?
COULD PAUL HAVE BEEN TRYING TO HELP ASH?
HUH!

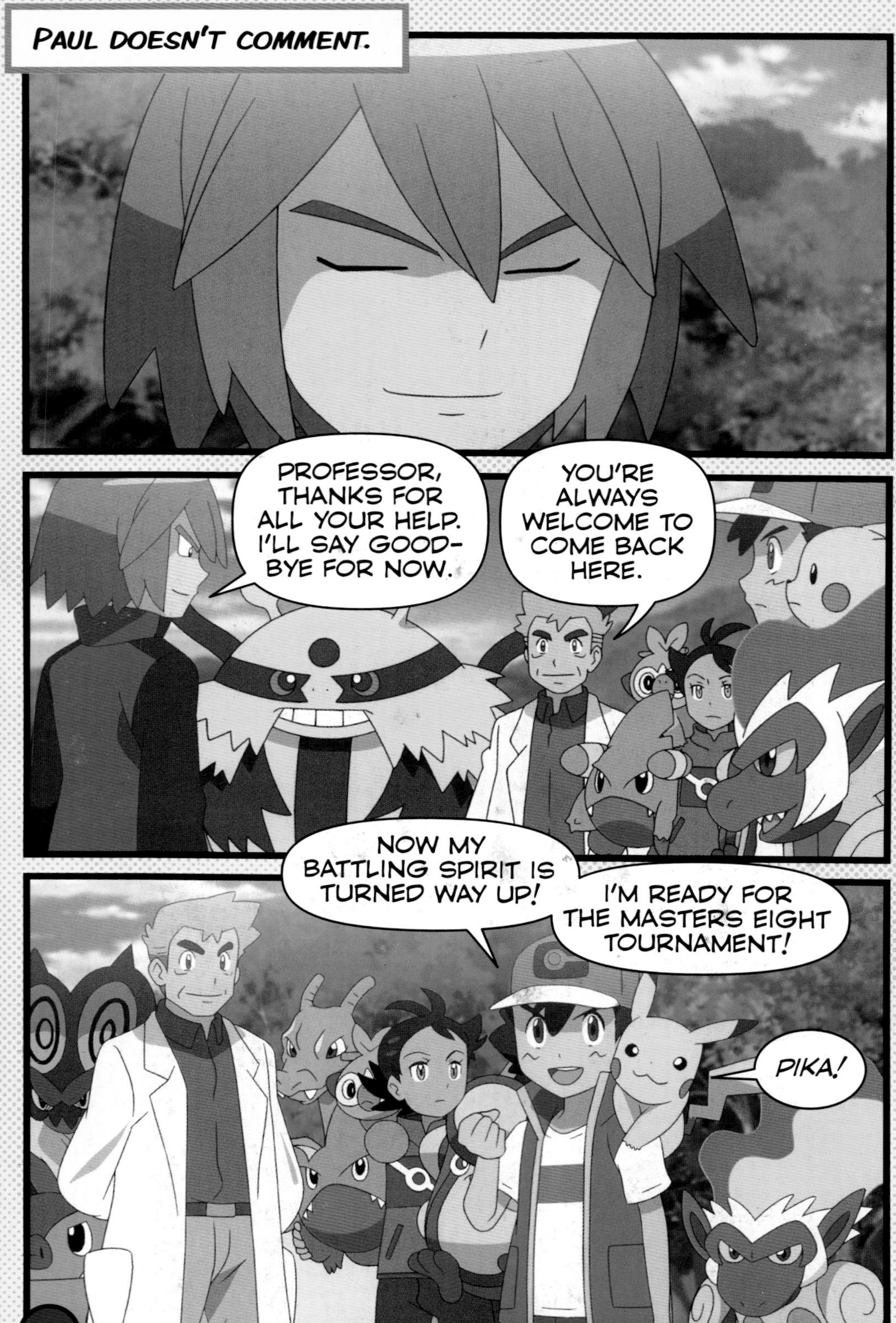
PAUL DOESN'T COMMENT.
PROFESSOR, THANKS FOR ALL YOUR HELP. I'LL SAY GOOD-BYE FOR NOW.
YOU'RE ALWAYS WELCOME TO COME BACK HERE.
NOW MY BATTLING SPIRIT IS TURNED WAY UP!
I'M READY FOR THE MASTERS EIGHT TOURNAMENT!
PIKA!